LUV
is a
Dirty Business
..still I like to go for it again

LUV is a Dirty Business

..still I like to go for it again

Shivansh kamra

Srishti
PUBLISHERS & DISTRIBUTORS

SRISHTI PUBLISHERS & DISTRIBUTORS
N-16, C. R. Park
New Delhi 110 019
srishtipublishers@gmail.com

First published by Srishti Publishers & Distributors in 2012

All the characters and incidences described in this book are a work of pure fiction. Any resemblance to any person dead or alive is purely coincidental.

Typeset in AGaramond 12pt. by Suresh Kumar Sharma at Srishti

Printed and bound in India

In the memory of my Grandpa Sri late Deshraj Jasuja

Acknowledgements

"I never knew a cup of coffee could actually do wonders for me. Someone once said randomly, Shiv why don't you write ". And those words got stuck in my mind. Here I am, Thanks to that someone (Aakriti Bansal) for being an inspiration and critic always. For making me realize that I can write more than blog. They say, without a reason one can't do anything and you were one of the reasons behind this. Thanks for listening to every single line I wrote from begining to end over the phone. Ah ! I know that wasn't an easy job for you.

Thanks to my parents who stood close to me and gave me all support. I would like to thank my Didi and Jiju for standing close to me and appreciate my decision.

Prerna Arora, Ah ! I will not thank you. Because I know you hate this word. But I will still say thanks to you for being an honest critic to the patient designer. For letting me torture you every now or then with my changing demands.

Samriti Sood, Thanks for reading the whole manuscript again and again. I actually made you read it thrice but you never said that you were bored or No ! Believe me that actually acted like a booster.

My publisher Srishti, for being so enthusiastic, professional and friendly all through the process. DA you simply rock!

Abhishek Jhamb and Amarbir Singh Mahal, for making the things easier and simpler for me.

You stood close to me when I felt thoroughly frustrated.

Sohail, my cousin and supporter. Thanks for giving me support at every phase. From begining to end. Your moral support and your belief that I can write gave me immense confidence.

See bro, I did it.

Saurabh Arya, Arpit Sharma, Mridul Sharma and Amrajot Singh kang. Thank you guys for all your support. Vipul Joshi, An intentional thanks to you for your unintentional help.

Last but not the least, Thanks to all those who never believed in me and thought I could never write. You guys gave me challenge and I hope I was up to the mark. I will wait for your calls.

Special thanks to some of my very close friends who stood close to me in later part. Thanks to Nitin, Aditya, Sonia, Amy, Sarika and Kevin.

WONDERS OF LIFE

Lollypops turn into cigarettes, innocent ones turn into fashion freaks; soft drink becomes alcohol, and kisses turn into sex. Remember when getting high meant swinging on the playground? When protection meant wearing a helmet? When the worst thing you could get from boys was cooties? Dad's shoulders were the highest and mum was your hero? Race issues were about who ran the fastest, the only drug you knew was cough medicine, and goodbye only meant until tomorrow, and yet all we wanted was to grow up fast.

But finally, when we find people calling us "Grown up Kids" then? We want to hit the rewind button of life. Just like if we can have Life Remote Control, Which will be having all the buttons which can make one's life interesting. Think about it, fast forwarding through all the monotonous junk of life. Pausing at nice moments and just relishing them, like a beautiful sunset, or a baby's smile. Skipping things like appearing in an exam, hangovers after last night's boozing. How cool would it be to replay all the great events of your life? Unless you have no great events, which is sad. Like once I went for a vacation to the mountains and I would love to press the replay button, and enabling myself to feel the freshness again. A slow motion button would also come into play, when I am on vacation and just enjoying it in a slow motion. And yes one more important button that would work and that is to mute all the things uttered by some teacher or maybe by the boss.

Just like I would love to delete the following incident.

Ah! Not again, tring tring of alarm, Oh no, It's been just two hours since I had entered my dream world, the clock was hitting two, my head was aching like hell, But yeah, It cannot be hangover, two hours since I had my last glass of beer.

Oh God Damn! It was Dev calling....

The moment I got myself to reality and managed to hit the answer button, an angry ugly voice of Dev hit my ears, which was the usual thing he did every time we booze.

"Nick, you know what man?" Dev said.

"Yup."

"Oh! Shut up." Dev said, loudly.

"Okay."

"My dad kicked me out of the house again, because I was drunk."

Before he could say anything more, I interrupted...

"Oh! Common, tell me something new."

"No, is this the way to treat with their only child?"

"I don't know."

"You know what? You are hopeless." he said.

"Thank you."

"Anyways, I am coming to your place." He said.

"No!" I said straightaway.

"What?"

"Because I am yet to open an orphanage."

"What the fuck!" Dev said.

"You are so irritating, you know that."

"Hmmmm....." Dev murmured about to shed crocodile tears.

"Oh! Don't start your melodrama again."

"Okay" Dev, low voice, but still an ugly one.

"Okay, you can give rest to your ass at my place."

"Thank you so much, I love you bro, muaaaaah...." Dev said happily.

"Now stop being gay dude and come."

And I hung up.

Well! Dev and I are virtual college mates. Virtual is a reference to our college, But yes, our frandship (Desi lingo) is more than real, at least for now, we were sharing the same bed. But now if I say, we are best friends, then its natural some of you, would make faces, just like when I said, we were sharing the same bed.

Why is it like that?

"Friends Forever" kind of thing is said only in between Girl-Guy

Guy-guy is only when they are drunk or gay, Right? I know it's weird but true.

It's been ages, since the last time we went to that 50 acre jail. It was the only first week after admission when we were prisoners out there and later we decided to get out of that jail, ever and forever, and yes, we are living happily ever after.

The only place, which I used to like in that jail was the cafeteria. You can call it a food plus babe treat, especially in summers, the icy cold coffee served with the long waxed legs of computers department chicks. Ice cream as feast for your tongue and the deep cleavage showing, feasting your eyes.

Sometimes I used to wonder, how could these chicks manage to do engineering and that too from this jail, in the end, what were they going to get?

- A prefix Er. with their name?
- Some going to marry as soon as this mission was accomplished.
- For some, professional suits were going to replace the mini skirt and short top.

Ah! How ridiculous it was! That was like, wasting beauty for the 17' by 17' square computer machine, wasting in encoding and coding of soft ware? How they really feel, seeing the refection of their cleavage on the computer screen? Don't they feel like hitting the ramp?

These questions do trouble my mind. Sometimes, I regret why I didn't choose computer engineering. And opted for that all boys mechanical department. Point to be noted here is that, I am talking about only SOME CHICKS.

· Name them? 32 '? 34 '? 36 '?

And we Mechanical department boys can find erotic things in this wide range of waists too, such as, Big round ass, curved ass and blah blah

But, there is a set of girls, who aren't that beautiful and not ready to accept the reality. Instead they try their level best to appear attractive. They are so dumb, that they can't even make out,

You can obviously buy and wear expensive clothes. But it's not the amount of money you spend on your clothes. It's the way u carry them. If you want to flaunt your body or cleavage, don't worry. Guys can scan you even if you are in burkha. Most of us know this thing, but still there are a few girls around who are such big turns off. They are like if they are screaming for attention and saying, "Hey, Want some?

Give us attention please. We want to show u attitude n all."

Believe me they look so fake as if one would look at their backs near the neck it says, Made in China.

In the last three years, I always had 100 % attendance in cafeteria and almost 0 % in real lectures, Even if musicians get together to create a melody to make me sleep! They can't beat the lecturers of my college! I have always been an alien to my class and teachers. The only time, I get into my class is every six months, That is, at the time of exams and in most of them, I got to see big "D "as suffix with my name, DETAINED!

BEGINNING OF DISASTER CALLED LOVE

A new morning, but everything was the same, centre table in cafeteria. Dev and me with our soft drinks, Limca, the reason being last night's boozing and not even a single word was exchanged for almost ten long minutes.

"So, what's next?" I finally uttered, breaking the silence.

"Don't know" Dev said, in an expressionless voice.

"It seems to be so empty today." I said.

"Yup, I guess all are in the auditorium, auditions are going on for the fest." He said.

"Oh! Okay, then what are we waiting for?"

"Let's go." Dev drained off the entire bottle of Limca.

"Where are you going guys?" Harsh asked, loudly.

Well! Harsh was the third member of our group, he was a little different from us, he was a committed brat, for the last two years, a little serious towards studies too, good with projects, But the good part was that, his girlfriend was in his hometown back in Himachal, so he never missed a chance, to catch a glimpse of those long waxed legs and deep cleavage.

But sometimes, I pity those committed guys, just like married men and committed guys. They don't belong to our breed.

I don't know WTF? Who invented this marriages and relationship thing? A guy goes stupid, He thinks too much... Pros and cons...

A typical guy/man is always in love for some new fun & committed/married ones are pleasing their girl friend/wives. If they try to live their own way, they get abused & cursed. If they live the girl's way, they lose themselves....Look at your single & committed friend. Analyze them.

Sometimes I used to think, how desperate tharkis we were. For us the quote "Cover the face, fuck the base" really suits. It was all about cleavage, navel and waxed legs, if it was all visible, then god damn, she was super hot; at least, I had this mindset.

"Auditorium, auditions are going on for fest" Dev answered Harsh.

"Oh! Fest, even I am thinking of making a presentation." Harsh sounded excited.

"Oh! That sounds cool!" Dev exclaimed.

"What about you Nick, why don't you go for a presentation or something?" Harsh asked.

"Yes, even I am thinking" I said

"What?" Dev sounded, surprised.

"Oh! Interesting, topic?" Harsh asked.

"Sexology." I said.

And they both laughed out loudly.

"And slides would be like, different positions of making love." I added.

"Are you kidding me?" Harsh said.

"Who started first?"

Well that used to be the only topic on which, most of our conversation revolved.

Nothing was so spectacular in the auditorium, some were trying to act like SRK in drama audition, and some were trying their level best with Sa Re Ga Ma Pa .... But I just couldn't understand what those dumb asses wanted to prove. Or maybe I was so dumb, that I couldn't make out what they were doing. But who really cared?

Being an ugly desperate soul, I resumed my search for hot chicks, starting from the music teacher to the drama one, to the computers one. But my lids got freezed at one point, It almost took my breath away, It made me speechless. All I can say that it was Grrr... She was....

The tresses of silky black hair lift neatly into a stunning pony. Her deep set of chocolate brown eyes looked at me like those of a puppy as she turned around to check what was going on at the back. She had a pixie like nose. Her cupid bow red lips surrounded her small mouth with perfect alabaster teeth. Dimples were pressed under high cheek bones; she had soft hands with long fingers terminated in painted, polished mauve nails. And finally, she stood at 5'5"and had a sensual figure.

Looking into her eyes and at her red lips, I found myself in her awe. The strange thing for me was that I was no more interested in spotting the breast line or in measuring the radius of her curves; it was her face which floored me that instance. I had never believed in love at first sight, but what was it? Even I didn't know, as all these thoughts were running through my mind, I saw her passing the Audi's gate, how time freezes? I thought of asking her name or may be her number, but all the stunts I thought of made me look dumb and dumber, finally she disappeared in the crowd and my eyes were still searching for her. It all happened so quickly that I just couldn't make out what it actually was. One can never say if it was love-at-first-sight or not but, admittedly the dent she left in my heart was a big one.

"Hey Nick" Heard a sweet voice from the corner of the exit gate, which was a rare thing for me. Oh! It was Samriti.

"Hey Hi" I said, with no real attention.

Samriti was the only girl in college who claimed to be my friend, unlike all other chicks, who always preferred to be friendly with those studious brats around.

"So, what's going on man?" Samriti asked.

"Damn, she has gone away." I said in a low voice.

"What? What happened? You seem to be lost somewhere" Samriti asked.

"Oh! Nothing... nothing."

"Okay!" Samriti with a straight look.

"Cafeteria?" I asked.

"Oh! Sure."

And we left the place. As we were on our way through common path, like always Samriti was hitting me with a hell of a lot of questions, how's it? How's that? Studies? Attendance? And my answers were roaming around Hmmm... Or Okay...., As my mind was still stuck to that enchanting beauty queen, I was looking for those chocolate brown eyes to glance at my face again..

Sometimes luck is a good dame, As we entered the cafeteria, I saw a girl sitting in the corner, she was having coffee, She had full lips and when she pouted, oh my god my heart shouted, "Yes she is the same girl" as soon as I managed to handle my emotions, I asked Samriti "Do you know that girl, The one in the corner."

"Which one? That yellow dress?"

"Yup."

"Oh! She is my junior, 3rd year computers."

"Oh!."

"What happened Nick? Why are you asking?" Samriti wanted to know.

"Nothing, just like that."

Actually that was the first time, When I really asked about some chick around, as always, I used to be a silent player, who just loved to see those deep cleavage lines, but never been into that flirting or love line.

"Sure?" Samriti made a query.

"Yeah, Anyways, Do you know her?"

"Oh! Yeah, she is Sneha, but I am sorry mate, she is not your type of girl." She said.

"Oh! Shut up."

"No, seriously, she is kind of studious girl; even I had a conversation with her once, that to related to project work only." She said.

"Expected, what else can you expect from her to talk about with a bookworm like you, boredom queen?"

"Errr... Nick I will kill you" Frustrated Samriti, as she always hated this tag.

"Okay kill me with your pen point."

"Okay, I am leaving, you can never change, you always, carry your bad boy image." She said with an almost red face

And she left the place, I always had "I don't give a damn attitude", it was different, that most of the times, it had acted against me.

"Nobody is good. I was not this bad. I am never bad, It's just I reflect the behavior which I get. With time understanding 'me' is getting tougher and complex. But no worries, I always have a way of enjoying myself because I don't die I multiply"

FACE BOOK: SEARCH: LOVE

Face book:

-Log on

-Check notifications

-Poke everyone back

-Go on homepage

-Do the "happy birthday" ritual

-Go back to homepage

-Have a little scroll down

-Like a couple of pages

-You're bored already...

The clock was showing ten, how bad addiction it was of Farm villa? Like my daily routine, I had never forgotten to harvest my farm or grow new crops; it was so damn unreal, logging into your face book account and then used to resume my fight for virtual farm and crops. While doing so, the name Sneha again struck my mind, and I started searching Sneha on Facebook account and luckily the first one out of the search result was she, the queen with 10 mutual friends. Again looking at her picture, I found myself in her awe.

She was wearing a red Esprit tee that clung to her best assets, a slight rip was that needed and the tee would have split all through, her skinny Levis showed off that ass, a million of girl would kill for.

And in no time, I added her as a friend, In split second she accepted my friend request and that actually gave me goose bumps like so unreal as if I had passed the whole semester in one go. Finally I managed to gather the courage to send her an IM.

Nikhil: Hey.

Sneha: Hi Sir.

Nikhil: Sir?

Sneha: Yes, I guess you are my senior.

In engineering College, juniors do call their seniors with a suffix Sir, Imagine, Nikhil Sir, Eh? How funny? But I liked it * Wink *

Nikhil: Oh! Right,

Sneha: Hmmm....

I was confused, what I should say. I want to know where she was from, what she likes. So that I could change what was wrong to right, if I made a move, would I be out of line?

10 minutes since we had last IM exchanged, finally it was she who made a move...

"Fest? "She asked.

That query of her made me go all blank, but later I decided to act a little studious.

"Oh yes, I am planning for a presentation."

"That's nice, Topic?" She asked

Sexology was the only topic, which could have slicked my mind; else I didn't know my subjects name even. Sometimes, when you have to lie, your mind starts working at 10x speed, and that's what happened to me.

"Working of computers "I said.

How disgusting was that, I was in Mechanical department and I was preparing for working of computers, but it was a computer only which I could see that time except Sneha's picture in other tab

"Oh! Really. Even I am planning for same."

"Great, if you don't mind we can team up, as I am yet to find my partner for that."

"Sure." She said

"Okay, 10 at cafeteria? "As I jumped of my bed, it was so unreal happening to me

"Okay" She said

"GTG, See ya, good night" She said

"Take care, Sleep well."

And she went offline, not bad Nikhil, I said it to myself. What's next? I was an alien to computers; I didn't know ABC of computers and working? Damn, no way near me. I kept on looking at that 22 minutes conversation and finally pinched myself to get in to reality, Oh! Yes, I really did it, which was so unreal for me, I was not afraid of what I was going to do with presentation but the one question, which was going through my mind was, How I was going to face beauty tomorrow?

With a sleepless night, a new morning, but it was not the same. I was going to meet her. As the clock struck 10, to my surprise she came on time. She was wearing a pink Tommy tee, with matching nail paint and her blackish Levis was showing off an ass a million of guys would go mad for.

"Hey!" I said.

"Hello Sir." As she seated herself on the chair.

"Can you please drop this 'Sir' for some time?"

"Sure." She took out a pen and a note pad from her pink bag.

"So how are you?"

"Good and you?" Still battling for something out there in bag.

If anyhow I had to utter the truth, I would say at that time, my heart was pumping faster, mind working at 10 x speed, I was very conscious of every move, as I just didn't want to lose the chance. Yes

I was feeling very excited.

"Doing great." I said

Oh! Those red lips, just felt like biting them, desperate me? May be yes, maybe no. But she had something else on her mind and that was the fucking presentation.

"So shall we start?" She asked me with a pen pointed on her notebook.

Oh yes girl, you too can, I had started my work the moment you came, damn, she was looking so hot.

"Okay." I said.

Too many thoughts were capturing my mind and finally I made my move...

"Look Sneha, I guess you need some experience, So you start with slides, if at any point you need my help I am there and don't disappoint me" I added.

What a fucking rascally statement it was! I am sure; it wasn't that bad to make an easy escape.

"Oh thank you so much sir, Oh! Sorry Nick." she smiled at me.

"Any time, After all we are friends, aren't we?" And my heart started throbbing hard again.

"Oh! Yes." She said.

Oh! Control yourself Nikhil, I said it to myself. It was all over for day one, numbers were exchanged. She was with me and the best part was that I did not have to rub my ass on that fucking presentation.

"Okay, I guess I must take leave now, got to attend the machine's lab."

One more move to give an impression of a fake studious brat, the weirdest statement I had ever made. If Dev had heard me, he would die on the spot of a heart attack.

"Okay, Take care." She said.

"Do give me a call, if there is any problem." I added.

OMG! What did she say? She asked me to take care, Oh! Yes, she had started caring for me. And with this my dreams soared again.

PRESENTATION, BUT I HAD NOTHING TO DO WITH IT

With a couple of telephonic conversation and with some 3-4 text chats, it was all about the real show. Just 12 hours and I was saddled with a fucking presentation. How disgusting it was! The most beautiful girl in the college would be sitting next to me and my work would be to press the enter button i.e. to change the slides. She asked me to go through the slides a night before and I just couldn't make out, what they were all about. From, hardware to software, mother board to load, coding to encoding, all shit and really I was not interested in it.

The good part in all this was that we were friends now, at least from my side.

Presentation day

Judgment day and it was presentation, I literally had no clue what was going to happen. My hands were sweating, I was short of confidence, I didn't know how I was going to face those mustaches, beards, specs, shirts, t-shirts, ties, black, blue, green, shaking heads, standing head, still heads, talking heads and dick heads, I had never faced such a situation before.

Sneha was late. As the time passed my nervousness level was reaching its peak. A nervous breakdown? Yes, quite possible. Finally she arrived. She was looking different today; she looked like a promising cover page model of women's wear. Her short black skirt, the white formal semi silky shirt clung to her best assets and her shiny black high heels completed the picture. In contrast to that my outfit, spiky hair as they were wrapped with gum, black US polo that had a horse around the chest line and skinny bluish Levis and white shoes, looked raw.

All this made me fumble,

"He... Hey.... Hey Sneha," Finally I managed to say.

"Hey! Nick," She took out a small mirror and started setting her smudged kajal right.

I had nothing to say, it was Sneha all over my mind. I was admiring her beauty, I was no more nervous.

Presentation... presentation.... for the last ten days, that was the only fucking topic which we had been discussing and It was all over, we did well, actually it was one woman show. It was Sneha who kept on speaking for those ten minutes. But yeah I did well in changing slides and was happy with that.

Organizers informed us that the results would be out in two hours. I was totally screwed up; I desperately needed a sutta break.

"Oh! I am tired now, let's go out." She said.

Oh! Yes baby, you must be tired, as you were running through my mind, all day long.

"Yes, let's go." I said.

We walked out together, that was the first time she was giving me so much attention. I was damn nervous. We crossed the road and before I could realize, she asked for a pack of Marlboro lights from the vendor, then took out a fluorescent lighter from her bag and did the needful, a small puff and a gush of smoke came out of her mouth.

"Nick, don't you smoke?" She asked me

"Oh! Yes, Classic regular." I demanded one from the vendor.

"Girls should not smoke, it's harmful." I advised her.

"And boys are allowed, isn't harmful for them as well Nick?"

"Why this discrimination?" She added.

Bad advice Nick, I said it to myself and thought of changing the topic. With normal chit chat, we completed our respective inhaling process.

"I guess results would be out by now." With that she took the last puff of her second cancer stick and squashed the butt.

"Oh! Yes."

One thing, I can say, I never said no to her. Maybe she was always right or maybe I never got to see anything wrong in her move.

The administrator announced the result and we had stood first. Hearing that, she came to me and hugged me with joy. I still can feel that first touch of her, the way she wrapped her naked long arms around my neck. That first touch! I almost had a 440 volt current in my body and that continued for 30 seconds. Finally she separated her silky body from mine.

"Yes we did it, we did it, and it's all because of you. Thank you so much Nick. You are lucky for me." She kept on screaming.

The hugging act, made me go all blank, my mouth was wide open. Was I surprised? Or my watery tongue was demanding for something more? Of course any moment, I wanted more. But why was she thanking me? She was the one who made the presentation and she was the only one who faced those scary creatures.

"No, Sneha. It's all because of you."

"No, Nick, you were with me always, and you are my lucky baby."

And that thing made our bond stronger; I was totally clueless, what was happening around? I turned out to be the lucky baby of the hottest babe around and Oh! Sure, I was lucky enough to have her around me.

SUCCESS PARTY

Okay this one, No... No.... this one will do? No..............!! Damn, I was so confused, what should I wear for the party, celebration party. With every possible permutation and combination I ended up wearing a pair of destroyed jeans, long inseam and slightly faded on the thighs, with a white slim fit Van Heusen shirt and a black coat.

F-Bar was the club on Saturday and the first one to turn up was Harsh. He was wearing a pair of blue jeans in orange stitch, looking good with white top and black waistcoat. For a change, this fat ass was looking good, but my eyes were searching for Sneha only, she was always late, except that first meeting. Later Dev joined us; He was wearing blue slim fit denim and complimented it with a light blue shirt and coat.

We were waiting for the girls to come, as Sneha was coming with her two friends.

Finally they arrived, like always, my eyelids were fixed on her. She looked stunning in her lequin black sequin mini. Her chocolate brown eyes were enhanced by long eyelashes that she flicked constantly. Her skin was slightly lighter than ivory, with a metallic rose colored tint to her cheeks. Her faultless hair fell loosely over her shoulder into skinny, slack curls. Her lips were like a rose, dangerous but beautiful.

Straight away she put her naked arms around my neck and whispered in my right ear that I was looking good. It was one of the memorable moments, the first time she had complimented me, and finally she pulled apart which I hated the most. I was more interested in feeling her around me.

"Well, this is Kashish and Sonia" she started introducing her friends.

Well! Kashish was looking lovely in her turquoise dress, while Sonia was shimmering in her icy silk maxi.

Dev – Kashish

Harsh – Sonia

Me – Sneha (Of course)

Finally, this combination worked for the couple entry inside arena. Now, we were in and she ordered 6 tequilas, the DJ was playing some tunes, which added to my excitement. With a countdown of 5, we all had our first shot, which was followed by 2 more, just 300 seconds and 3 shots were in. By then I could feel something in me, I was somewhat more relaxed and was finding it easier to strike up a conversation. On the other hand, Sneha was coming out of her shell and was getting free with me, yes for sure, Shots were doing their work. In reality, by now, we cared least about our mates out there.

One more shot, but this time, it was Sneha and me only. As that 10 ml transparent liquid entered my food pipe, I could feel an urge of getting closer to her; maybe she was feeling the same.

"OH! God, I love it. " As she reapplied her lippy.

"Ahan?" trying to make an eye contact with her.

And she gave me a raised eyebrows look, it was her feisty style and I simply loved it, when she looked at me that way. DJ was playing her favorite song; again I loved the way she was beckoning to me to dance.

Closer, closer, dancing made hormones go on a high, the way she was teasing me, pulling me, pushing me, we almost kissed each other, but again it was her teasing act, but we wanted more...

One more shot and I knew we would be out, but that was what we actually wanted, at least me, My urge to feel her around me was reaching its peak, But before, we could have more, She said "Nick let's go out, I am feeling high."

With a little walk to parking area, we seated our self in my car, doors were closed, black filming and we were all alone That day I felt the importance of black filming, no one could look into your private area, No one to disturb, we could hear our fast breathing. And she held my hand, I was all again nervous.

"Are you alright now? "I asked and she nodded.

Getting closer to her, holding her hand, closer and it was all happening. And I planted a kiss on her forehead and she rested her head on my right shoulder and my hands were caressing her back. With an eye contact we exchanged our unsaid feelings and got closer to her, almost close to her red lips. I could feel her fast breath and with a little bit on her upper lip, I took a step forward, which ended in a passionate kiss. My upper lip, her upper one, my lower lip, her lower one, pushing and more pushing and more pushing, played with tongue, the taste of her saliva with a combo of her lipstick was the best meal I could ever had. With an exchange of some oooo and aaaas, screwed her with every bit of energy I could spare. We finally made it and I kissed her nose.

And that kiss. I now know why, nobody named how lips taste. No, it was not sweet, not something shocking. It was so subtle, very slow; the taste of her lips in the kiss was ethereal. And when she smiled after that, that was when the taste grew better.

A CHANGE

I feel like kicking her ass, seriously man it sucks, the bloody computer operator, *"The number which you are trying to call is currently switched off"* a big time fucking statement. I have been trying to call Sneha for the last two hours, but why the hell her phone was switched off. With a sip of coffee, scratching my head, worried. I just couldn't make out, why? Why? Why her phone was switched off? She hates me now after last night's incident? Was she having some regrets? She is feeling guilty? Ignoring me? All such fucking thoughts were hitting my mind, I was clueless, and one part of my mind was saying, "Calm down Nick! May be, there is some network problem, May be .... Something... something ... " But the other part was giving me fucking negative thoughts, before I could think more, She came up to the scene, I asked her straight away ...

"Sneha, I have been trying to call you since morning, why is your phone switched off."

"Oh! I forgot to charge it " She said.

"I was tensed and worried."

"Common Nick! Take a chill pill."

I just can't understand what the fuck this chill pill is? She seemed to be pretty normal, as if nothing had happened between us, I was quite surprised with her behavior, and she was kind of expressionless. A normal chit chat and she left the place, and again and again... The same story, she used to come, a normal chit chat and used to leave.

Was she my girl friend? Was she my friend? A one night stand friend? A presentation partner or what?

I was damn confused about our relationship, because I just couldn't make out anything from her moves, the only change was that, now we were having good long telephonic conversation, but again the same thing, she was normal.

She called up at eleven forty, late as usual. But I didn't mind that, in fact I kind of liked that. Coming late, taking hours to dress, Yes, sometimes when your mood is not good, these get on to you, but mostly I used to smile inwardly and marvel at the uniqueness and beauty of her charms. It was good to talk to her late at night. We lost all sense of time and surroundings and become completely lost in each other; suddenly one of us glanced at the watch and realizes we had been taking for two hours.

Shall I propose to her? Will she say yes or a no? All these thoughts were of passing through my mind, but was there proposal really required? We had sex; she had given me her most precious thing,

In some of our telephonic conversations I tried to let her know, what I felt for her, and when I finally had the courage to say "I LOVE YOU". She just said, "You're really funny! That's what I like about you because you are the funniest friend ever!!!!" But again either she ignored those senti talks or gave me that fucking philosophy. Look Nick, Isn't it enough we are together? And blah blah

Even I used to think sometimes. She was with me and I knew she was not going around with someone else, then why to hurry? Let the time decide.

Now, the relationship between me and Sneha was growing day by day, we were getting to know each other, her likes and dislikes, even I told her everything about my degree status, that I still had 6 papers to clear from previous semesters.

And it goes on.....

8AM...phon's ringing, "I bet it is my baby, Sneha!!" *look at phone*, "Fucking telemarketers"!! Ugh

She used to wake me up on those chilly mornings and sometimes I used to. Those good morning greetings, weekend movies, parties and yeah last but not the least, she used to make me study. She was the one, who made me understand, what life really was? The ups and downs and in the end it's all about your education, which is going to help you to survive.

Now, It was all changed, I started attending lectures, but yes I was still managing my cafeteria attendance too. There was something which was constantly building and developing in my heart and mind. It was Sneha who used to capture my heart most of the time, May be I was falling for her. Every time, I thought about her, every time, I fell in love with her. Every time I saw her, my heart ran out of me to serve her. I didn't know how to react; I never felt the same for any other girl. Love was showing its magic on me and changing me, I was sure about my love for her, but was not sure what was in her mind. It was one of our normal telephonic conversations and I said

"Sneha, I want to say something."

"Go on." She said.

"I guess I am falling for you."

2 Minutes silence, then she laughed out loudly

"What Nick? You are falling?"

"Yes."

"Oh! My baby, then get on to your bed, how can you fall from it?"

"Shut up!"

"Okay."

Again, she ignored it.

After this, I never really tried to let her know about my feelings; I guess Samriti was right, as she said "She is a career conscious girl, and she will never go with a spoiled brat like me."

One sided love with a one night stand, I guess, It was the script of my story. In last six months, she came so closer to me but yet so far. I turned out to be her bestie, but was yet to get that boy friend tag. I used to get those rare "muwahzZzz "from her in messages and those were enough for my love to grow up.

Like my image you must be thinking I was more interested in looking at Sneha's ass,
I am more interested in what's behind her glasses.
Erotic looks, a sensual glance,
my mind wanna get up and dance.
There is nothing more than a completely loving stare,
looking into each other's eyes,
Nothing in life is so fair.
The big round eyes, with the deep black looks,
those are the ones that are on my books.
I'd rather look into your glazing glare,
Than screw you with energy I can spare,
but sure enough, the more erotic the look,
you'll be adding another number in your little black book.

I could make out one thing that she wasn't seeing her future with me, as I had no real hopes of getting a good placement. In my life I had never felt that I should study or learn something. Life had always been a joyride, fun n frolic.

Sometimes classes can be such a waste of time. There are so many more important things to be done. All I want is a workshop with a machinist and a welder. It's so amazingly frustrating when one is standing around with material and work to be done yet can only look at the walls because one must wait for tools or a machine. So much to do, so little time. We know we can never really love something till you build every bit of it with your hands, till you cut burn and electrocute yourself building it, till you know each and every inch of it like the back of your hand. Nothing beats working with your hands and when it's almost complete and your baby stands all by itself for the very first time, there are no words to describe the feeling.

But for the first time I feel like studying more and grasping more and more knowledge. I feel like I want to know more, not because that will get me more money. But I feel a sort of craving for knowledge. This craving is something.

And this thought actually made me clear my entire backlogs in just one go, by the eighth semester. I must say that it was not at all a bad show; I was kind of feeling proud of myself, one step closer to Sneha. More than me, it was Sneha who was flying high.

But my work was not yet over; I still had to pass the biggest hurdle called getting placed. I desperately wanted to get placed. And I was not confident enough. Would I get a job or not? But like always Sneha stood next to me, she gave me some aptitude test books and did everything possible to boost me. Our dates turned out to be the biggest boosters for me.

The best thing in life is finding someone who knows all your mistakes and weaknesses and still thinks you are absolutely amazing.

AN UNOFFICIAL DATE

It seemed to be all perfect. But there was something which did not seem all right. What was it? I didn't know. She was with me, a cup of coffee and sometimes a cup of coffee can add so many flavors to love and I was just hoping for that to happen. But like always every thought used to end with a 'but.' I was already flowing in her love but again it was Sneha who was not making a move to take a step forward or maybe she was not ready for it. Whatever it was, I loved admiring her beauty. Every time I saw her, my heart went out to serve her.

Her dark hair fell like a curtain of silk to her waist, the sunlight catching the stray strands that blew across her face. In a way this made her appear more beautiful, as her chocolate brown hair complimented her eyes which were of a similar shade. Her eyes were without doubt the most captivating aspect of her face, reflecting a look of wisdom that could not help but draw people. She did not care much for makeup, favoring an instead neutral look to compliment natural beauty. Her tanned skin and tall, slender build was like that of a model's and with the trendy dresses she wore, she gave the impression that she had just stepped off a runway.

Lips were full and sort of pouted when she wasn't smiling. When she did, her teeth were evenly distributed and as white as newly fallen snow. Everything about her was perfect, right down to her luscious figure, the faded jeans and the red tee.

"What separates you and me on this date is a cup of hot steaming coffee." She said settling down.

"You know what; the concept of coffee belongs to the era bygone." I said.

I picked up a ping pong ball from my pocket and pushed it from my end to hers. Ah! She gently pushed it back. I did the same. As the ball moved from side to side

I just saw her giving me a killer smile. But suddenly, Sneha gave the ball a Sania Mirza forehand. Oh! It was something different for me.

Indeed I felt like a pilot who had put his flight on auto pilot mode. A pilot, who was a little laid back, was taking a nap and was slightly taken aback. Ah! My forehand went in vain. And the ping pong ball went off the table.

She started celebrating like Kim Clijsters did after lifting the US open. And I was like John Mcenroe throwing tantrums. My ego got burnt, I was a little hurt.

Unusual date you can say, with a bizarre experience. In my defeat I could smile as she was smiling, may be that was my love for her which actually was still an alien thing for her. Or maybe she was pretending. To cool things off and bring in a little more peace I ordered two mugs of coffee.

I looked into her eyes and so did she. Ah! Again she gave me a killer smile. Although for a second, but it felt simply awesome. The first time we shared a glance. I knew it, I felt it actually. It was my only chance. But I could feel the nerves. Oh! I was nervous and scared too especially after the ping pong ball encounter.

Looking at the ground, she opened her lips but said nothing. Ah! I thought I had made it, a beat, my heart just skipped. But still I was clueless about my next move. And over the table besides the tray, my hand made a move towards her hand. But she withdrew her hand. I withdrew mine too. A withdrawal by her was assuring with an expression that reflected consent. It was all a pretense.

"So what else? Have you met Dev?" She asked.

"I was supposed to but he couldn't come."

"Why?" Shocked as if I had missed an exam.

"He had a date."

"With Whom? New Girl?"

"Off course, He never sticks to one, you know him."

"Oh! Not again. First time I have seen such a materialistic and unemotional guy."

"Why?"

"No, Look at him. His life roams around brands, jeans, tees, bikes, cars, accessories. Seriously, disgusting."

"And new girlfriends." I added to the list.

"Oh! Yeah. A new girlfriend every other month, you can say."

"An important one."

"No, at some point of life one has to stop that, right?"

"Well! I am happy to stick at one"

"Who?"

"You."

"Oh! Really Nick?"

"Yes."

"Shut up! Nikhil Arora bread ka pakora. Stop flirting with me."

"First, I am not flirting. Second, I am not a pakora."

"Okay."

Perhaps I really love her. What then?! Wow. I love her hands; they are tender, like a baby's. Wow. I love her feet, they are so pink. Wow. I love her cheeks; look at them when they blush! Wow. I love her eyes. They are so soft and endlessly deep. They almost smile at me, her eyes. Wow. I love her hair. They smell so beautiful when I hug her. Wow. I love her lips. Wow. Perhaps I do love her, but I have no way of telling her.

I loved the way she teased me. Knowing everything she used to act like an innocent baby. Oh! Jesus save me, I am falling for her. Ah! Those lips and when she pouted. I thought of making a move again towards her hand, touching her finger tips, but I didn't. May be I was scared that she might withdraw it again.

Literally I could feel sweat on my palms. I could see myself falling for her beauty. For a second, I felt like standing tall, holding her hand, pushing her towards me, wrapping my arms around her waist and hugging her. But that didn't happen. Yes, finally I stood tall but only in later part, when it was time to leave.

Come on! Smiles, kisses, giggles, hugs and some more giggles. Where has my darned life come to? The two of us were laughing, discussing the good old jokes of Tony and Dhoni.

PLACEMENT

If she is amazing, she won't be easy.

If she is easy, she won't be amazing.

If she worth it, you won't give up,

If you give up, you are not worth it.

Failure! Failure and again a failure.... five companies in a row and I failed to clear even a single test. Going for the interview round was still an alien thing for me. I was yet to appear for the interview round.

I had never paid attention to my studies, how could I expect getting placed in one go. Oh! Yes, I was not the hero of some Bollywood movie. With so many failures under my belt, I started losing all my confidence which Sneha managed to develop in me. Getting frustrated and irritated were part of my mood by then. But every time, I used to see Sneha, I used to forget all my failures. Her broad smile used to act like an energy booster for me.

Friday morning it was and like always it was me and my centre table in the cafeteria and Sneha came in shouting.

"Oh! Yes... Oh! Yes... Nickkkk this is your last chance, go for it."

"What?"

"Yes, a company is coming for placement on Monday."

"So what?"

"I am sure this time you are going to make it."

"But I don't think so, I had better be jobless."

"Oh! Common, don't talk like this. Clear it for me."

Damn! I literally hated her for that. The emotional atyachar. But then I thought, Okay Nick, Let's face one more rejection, let's see how worst feeling it could be.

"Okay." I said.

English, Grammar, Reasoning based questions. Damn they were pissing me off. Passing the aptitude test was a big thing for me, one more weekend spoiled in those bloody books. It was Sunday night. Still I had no hopes of clearing the test. But somewhere down the line I desperately wanted to pass the exam. But again it's not all about desperation man. With so many random thoughts, some negative - some positive I fell asleep.

Monday Morning, A blue shirt and gray trousers, black shoes. A formal look for the sixth time. One more rejection, Failure or I will pass? It was really my last chance to get a job or to get Sneha in my life.

Somehow, I managed to do well in the test. With the experience of the previous five appearances I managed to attempt some twenty questions out of thirty. But again I was not sure whether I would pass or not. As I passed my answer sheet to the invigilator, she told me, "Results would be out in 30 minutes or so."

Altogether they selected 40 students and Guess what? The 40th one was Nikhil Arora. Oh! Damn. Finallyyyyyy... I cleared the test but the real show, the interview was still left.

"Interviews will be conducted after the lunch break." Someone from admin announced.

In no time I called up Sneha.

"Oh! Yes, I cleared it; I cleared the first round." I shouted.

"Congratulations baby."

"Thank you so much."

"Where are you right now, let me join you?"

"Placement cell."

One step closer to job means one step closer to Sneha. I was again feeling confident, cheered up, boosting energy. I was getting a bit nervous regarding the interview round.

Just be yourself. Be confident. Don't fumble. Stay calm and blah blah. While Sneha was giving her lecture regarding the interview round, I was constantly looking at her, looking at those chocolate brown eyes, black eye lashes, for a moment I almost forgot that I had an interview in 30 minutes. I was no more nervous but confused. I was confident, but not overly. I knew if I got the job she would be mine. Like a day dreamer, I started thinking about the ways to propose to her instead of thinking about the interview. Pinched myself, Common Nick, Get back to reality and concentrate on fucking interview.

INTERVIEW

A small cabin. A middle aged nerdy guy was sitting on the round table, it was the HR round.

Int: Hello, Nikhil Arora, right?

I: Oh! Yes. Good afternoon sir. (Fake smile)

At first instance, looking at that fat ass, I kind of judged that he was never going to select me.

Int: Okay, tell me something about yourself.

I: I am Nikhil Arora. I was born and raised in Delhi.... Blah blah...

Damn the basic information. It was all written on my file but actually nothing else came to my mind.

I: Well! I believe nothing comes in life as a piece of cake; you need to reach out for what you want.

Oh! Of course, Sneha was not a piece of cake for me and I was trying my level best to get her, Appearing for a job interview was part of it.

I: Academically I am a student who likes to be challenged mentally and I enjoy both hands on projects as well as on conventional learning.

I must admit, I was lying at my best, Projects, Studies and Academics? I was no way near that. But this was my fakeness talent show.

I: yes we cannot change our destiny but we can surely learn to live with whatever comes to us.

I was just making my statement true, like the way that fat ass was throwing his fucking questions on me; I was just giving him back.

Int: okay nice.

I smiled at him again.

Int: Why should I hire you?

I: Well! This is the start of my professional career. So I want to take this job as a stepping stone and can see myself working for the same after 5 years from now.

Yes. I wanted that job as a stepping stone of my LOVE life.

Int: Okay, thank you.

With greetings I came out of the burning hot cabin.

Success or failure? Random thoughts were running in my mind. While I was waiting for results, someone called me?

As I went in, the lady in red gave me some forms to fill. I had no clue what that was for.

Name: ....

Father's Name:..................

Percentage: ....

As I just passed the three columns my hands froze for a second after the bold letter heading of the form and it said "Employee's Information" I got stuck to the word "Employee". Am I Selected? Oh! Common, don't tell me that fat ass finally saw the spark in me, but later the lady confirmed that "I had been selected Congratulations."

Oh My God! I passed it, yes I did it. WhoooHhhoo! I felt like jumping high in the sky. Somehow, I managed to fill the fucking form with shaking hands. I was damn curious to show my call letter to Sneha. "Yes now she will be mine."

After having five in row failures under my belt I finally managed to get one. I got the job. Sneha was damn happy when I told her about this; she hugged me and planted a kiss on my right cheek. Her fragrance filled my breath. She came so close to me. But again that was for a split second. I could sense that she would be there for me forever and ever to love me.

PLOTTING THE PLAN OF LOVE

"I try and try, but no matter where life takes me, I always end up thinking about you."

Shall I propose her? No you need to make it special man ... Farewell?

Don't we all take it easy; I say what I feel like. I do what I want. I am just my own person somehow. Is it too much to ask, when I say I want someone to care for me to give me joy and happiness or is too much to ask when I say get onto a random friend whom I can have fun with... wonder if the word crush makes more sense or the word LUST!

Lying on bed and such thoughts were running in my mind, looking at her picture in my cell phone and talking to her. I used to love those talk sessions. But don't know from where, Dev and Harsh came on the scene as they entered my room and spoiled our secret session, shouting....

"Damn! I can't believe you got the job?" Dev said and jumped on my bed and I was feeling bad for the bed sheet as stinky Dev was on it.

"What do you mean by YOU?"

"I mean how can they select you? Who doesn't even know the basics of Mechanics?"

"Yeah Nick, the cafeteria master the one who knows how to glance at those cleavages in every possible manner, But mechanics? Naaahhh" the fucking statement Harsh made, but true.

"Oh common, you losers, shut the fuck up."

"No seriously tell me, how?" Harsh said.

"Don't tell me, you allowed him to fuck you. Casting couch, is it?" Dev said and passed his not so heartening laugh.

"No actually I fucked that fat ass and that too with my words."

And we laughed out loudly.

"Anyways, Nick. Now what about Sneha? Did you tell her about your feelings?" Harsh switched on my computer.

"No."

"What?" Harsh was almost shocked.

"Don't be so surprised Harsh, This is what we can expect from him. You know what? You are as useless as the "H" in "John" I doubt if you have balls, Right Nick?" Dev said.

Dev and his taunting quotes, I always hated them to the core.

"What? Just wait and watch. Farewell party ... And she will be mine."

"We will see." Dev said with hilarious expressions.

Farewell party? Damn! I didn't know from where the hell I made this fucking statement but I had no other option to shut his mouth. But I had a job in my hand. My process of adding prefixes Er. to my name was almost over. It was all perfect but seemed to be so much imperfect without Sneha.

There was no real change in Sneha's behavior towards me; those friendship philosophies and blah blah were still on. Unlike my expectations she was behaving so normally. I was expecting her to show at least a little bit of feelings but again it was not there. But I had one thing very clear in my mind and it was that I was going to propose her on farewell night."

I don't know why but she started ignoring me, No more long phone calls, no more parties, no movies and the reason she gave me was that she wanted to concentrate on studies as exams were approaching. Oh! Okay... I didn't know exams were approaching. But one month was still left, then why? Irritation and frustration were part of my mood by then. A day without listening to her was turning out to be a horrible one but that was actually happening on a regular basis now. Respecting her decision, somewhere down the line I was hurting myself. More than my studies, I found myself lost in her thoughts and speculated on the ways to propose to her, thinking about her. The way she smiled at me, I was losing myself. Every time I called her, it was either on voice mail or some ring ring.

What was actually happening? I didn't know. Like always, she and her behavior was mysterious. She never opened her cards to me.

"Do not disturb me. I am studying." She finally messaged me in reply to my 50 calls. Later I thought, I shall stop irritating her, Let her study.

Was she a bookworm? Actually no. She never forgets to update her facebook status, but where was I? May be nowhere, May be in her heart and again too many thoughts. I wanted her to show the clueless love but did she ever love me, May be? I will get my answers on farewell night.

FAREWELL!

"Okay this looks cool" As I adjusted my tie in front of that small mirror in the men's washroom. It was Friday night. It was mid April and more importantly it was our farewell night. It was beautiful, full moon, stars adding to the glitzy sky. But still the long road from the cafeteria to the lecture hall which had in it four years of great memories that had made it beautiful. Those long walks with Sneha. Now that we couldn't come back it wouldn't be the same we would no longer be a part of the road, the cafeteria and the college. My four years had been eventful but my college had nothing to do with it. It was all about the cafeteria, those feasting cleavages, the samosas and ketchups. I hadn't made a lot of friends as most of them were not of my type. Some tried to sweet and friendly with you because, they thought you were more impressive or being friends with you will make them cool or something like that. That's the reason I am not sweet to all the people I know. I am just way I am. I'll be up the whole night when you need me. Can be a genie to support you in bad-good situations and can be bad enough to spit on you. I am not bad, but I don't like being GOOD to everybody

Harsh, Dev and the bookworm Samriti, I just managed to say hello to them. In 4 years, may be Sneha was the best and worst thing that happened to me in later part.

The farewell was great on eyes, so was Sneha. She was wearing a beautiful pink saree; she was looking like a goddess. She had applied kajal to her big expressive eyes, little mascara and her face was shining brilliantly. She looked like an angel from the heaven, her long hair was constantly coming in front of eyes and every time she flicked it across but the mischievous hair wanted to kiss her soft lips. She looked busy with the organizing stuff as she waved at me, letting me know that for a change I was looking good.

The evening was not that spectacular except those glances which she would give me each moment. We were yet to exchange a word but we had said a lot through those mysterious glances. After all the dancing and the nick name session got over, people bounced on food. It always tastes better when there is no bill following it. Harsh and Dev were finding difficult even to stand straight. Despite of free food and whiskey I was not feeling good actually I was very nervous, because I was going to propose the most beautiful girl out there.

One thing that left me keep wondering that if these girls can actually look so good then why don't they do it every day? What was so special about that night? Anyways, I was interested in only Sneha and she was looking beautiful as ever.

Was I ready? Yes actually I was. I did my homework. I had no idea what was going to happen, but I made my mind clear that I was going to tell her what I fell for her. From top to bottom she had changed me and I loved the change. But her love was the only missing thing.

"Hey, where are you going?" A voice called out from behind as I was I was walking down the corridor and it was Sneha.

"For a walk."

"Oh! I better join this lonely soul." She teased me.

A silent 100 meter walk and then I said...

"You are looking beautiful tonight."

I made my first move, complimenting her, like every girl loves admiration and she was no different.

"And pink really makes you look gorgeous." I added.

"Oh! Thank you so much. But I thought you don't like traditional ones." She said as she adjusted her saree.

"No! I love everything when it comes to you."

"Oh! Nick stop flirting."

"I am not flirting; it's called a conversation with the opposite sex."

"Okay I see." And she laughed at me.

I am mistaken for a flirt when I am friendly. I am mistaken for a dog when I am blunt. I am mistaken for sad when I am alone. I am mistaken for shy when I am quiet. Quit assuming and get to know me.

A beautiful girl can make you feel dizzy like you have been drinking jack and coke all morning. She can make you feel high full of the single greatest commodity known to man. Promise - Promise of new tomorrow. In her smile, in her soul, the way she makes every rotten little thing about life, like it's going to be okay. In my case it was Sneha. She had changed me from spoiled brat to an average student, from a hungry horny soul to Man in love. I had so much to say. But words were not coming out. I was nervous.

Walking on the path from campus to cafeteria I felt like holding her hand, but couldn't. A cool breeze was flowing whispering in my ears "Yes Nick, go ahead" and somehow I managed to gather the courage and said …

"Sneha I want to say something."

"Hmmm..." She seated herself on the road side bench as maybe she was feeling a little tired of walking.

Like an age old way of going down on knees, I said.

"Sneha you know that I like you, is it love or infatuation? I really have no clue. But my heart beats for you. You were the one who changed me, taught me how to love. Every time I see your face my heart takes off on high speed chase."

She interrupted me and said...

"Thank you and yes Nick we are kind of friends." She smiled at me.

Kind of friends? Yes we were kind of fucking friends only... Boohoo.

"But Sneha, Now is the time when we should take a step forward, don't lie to yourself, don't you care for me? Don't you like me? Don't you...."

Before I could say anything, she said with face without a smile.

"Look Nick, Let me make everything clear, isn't that enough I am with you? Why do you want more? Why do you want a boy friend girlfriend tag? You yourself said you like me, like me, I don't have any problem. Even I like you but relation? I am sorry. That's not for me, I just can't bear it."

"But what was that?" Still down on my knees.

"What? Oh don't tell me you are talking about that party accident."

"Accident?"

"Yes accident or to be precise one night stand, I don't even remember what happened that night. I was high so just forget about that thing."

"What.... But.... you ....."

"Oh! Common, Shut the fuck up! I am leaving."

And she left.

Still down on knees, more than my knees, I could feel pain in my heart. I didn't even get a chance to show her the ring and that remained as a mare spectator in my pocket. Looking at the bench, I was still trying to find her, but she had gone away. I had no place to hide. My soul was crushed. My heart was shattered. My eyes went dry. The thoughts were empty. I saw myself helpless and lame. But all I could do was think lonely, was she a stranger or she was the same? My face was numb, the tears were silent, and I didn't know if I should be calm or violent. The world came crashing down and I didn't even get a chance to shed my tears, I was not able to believe how things had changed and it seemed like I was on a boat which was far from the shore. All the things I thought of got ruined in one go, there was nothing called we or us. It was all alone me, just this feeling.

Don't know if it is feeling good or feeling betrayed. But rage fills my heart. It flows through my veins into my soul, the pain. It is infused right into me. The hurt mind is wandering, and starting to blot out my thoughts. My tears, thoughts, ambitions all strummed along as though they were a biotic. The sad tone, darkness filling the depth, the smell of violet, the accumulated force in my fist, the song playing in my ears, the numbness in my feet, the black smell of sweat, this is when reality is an illusion. Or at least I feel so. Sweetly sprayed around, scattered all over, my thoughts, my pain are soothed over a dried rose. The scent no more, the dead petal oozes everything but does not care. Wrinkled, folded and dead. The rose is alive no more. The bright streak of grit turning around me, all over me. Burns my eyes, enlightening my soul. Or does it? All the while, the dry patch in my throat, craving for some liquid, a new lease of life, a fresh breath, new blood, a finished soul. Or were they new?

DEAD ME

Life is nothing but an endless 'coma' & 'colon' with a full stop only being when one is hurtled into nothingness.

Here I am... lost in the ashes of time. But who really wants tomorrow? The noise posses no sound, the colors were no longer mine. It was true I was sad. It was true I was blue.

Why do we feel pain? Why isn't there the medication of some pains and feelings? Why does air becomes heavy and you know that you have to take it in, there is no other choice.

It was strange, I didn't know her, it was strange, and she was a stranger. We got together so well as if we had always been together. The start was never a beginning. But seemed like joining roads. The way was never new; it soon started to get dark. With no rays of hope the day seemed to end so fast, as if it had seen nothing.

I somehow feel like a lost soul, empty and hollow; I feel I have somehow lost my existence yet again. And have to live with this feeling of emptiness and keep falling into this bottomless pit till someone pulls me out. But somehow even then I know I shall keep falling as my physical body shall be out but my soul will be right there in the middle of that pit aching for that care and love I missed out on each and every time.

No college, No more cafeteria, No friends. But all I could do was to think how lonely I was, constantly thinking about her, had the addiction of texting her every next minute, but it was all changed and ended up checking my phone constantly. I loved her, but she never loved me.

It was all changed. No more telephonic conversations. No more texting. No parties. *Asking myself why I keep on loving you? When it's clear that you don't feel the same way for me, The problem is that I can't force you to love me, I can't force myself to stop loving you.*

Exams were approaching but I had no plans of hitting the books, everything around me sounded so meaningless. Days were okay as most of the time I used to sleep. But nights, they were horrible. Insomnia was the disease and I was turning on to be an insomniac. Covers pulled over me, yet sleep looked alike a distant dream, Gazing at the sky, listening to my own sigh. There were some positive things which happened to me; I had a job, an all clear degree but literally no reason to stay happy. I tried to contact Sneha. *I was always connected online hooked on facebook all the time hoping she checked my profile, may be its true I was caught up on her maybe there was a chance that she was stuck on me too.*

I drove my car NOW and closed the windows and freaking screamed, yelled, and cried. That is what I wanted to do for the past 6 days. That is what I wanted to do each moment I lost me.

"Oh! Come on, this is not the end of life, I know you are broken But just tell me, by doing this what would you get? You are just ruining your life. Will she ever come back?" Grinding the crispy uncle chips between his molars harsh said.

"No." he said.

"Life is a bitch so be a dog and fuck it. Never knock on death's door, ring the bell and run away, death really hates it." Dev said.

Well! It was least expected from Dev but he really acted sensibly. With hell of a lot of boosting efforts they finally managed to lift me a little. Yes a little. I smiled a bit, but somewhere my heart was still feeling the pain.

Was I pretending to be happy? Maybe yes. But that didn't mean that everything was perfect, it meant that I had decided to look beyond imperfection.

While I was passing through that phase, I came across Sneha twice in college, She seemed pretty normal with the goings. I had no courage to look into her eyes even as she passed me. Sometimes I used to think "Just because she comes off strong doesn't mean she didn't fall asleep crying, even though she acts like nothing is wrong, maybe she's just really good at lying." But somewhere I had accepted the truth that she was history by now.

Final Exams of Final Year…

Study.....Stud.....Stu....St..............S.............Sl.......Slee.................Sleeep...

It was actually like this, I was no more interested rubbing my ass with books, but literally I had to. A new life was waiting for me, a job adventure. But it was the exams hurdle which I had to clear first. Trust me; it was really a difficult job to be done. Study with a break up around the corner. I had missed her like hell, the way she used to make me study. Somehow I managed to do well in exams. Five out of six went good. It was last exam, Last time I was going to appear in that examination hall in my college life. It was a bit of an emotional moment too. The entire period of four years was running across my mind. But I really wanted an escape from that place, because it used to remind me every single thing about Sneha and was making it more difficult for me. I don't get how a heart can be so broken. I don't get how a mind can be so confused. I don't get how a smile can stay upside down for so long. I just don't get it.

After my last battle with mechanical drawing, for once I thought of approaching Sneha for one last time but I didn't. Maybe I had no real hopes, maybe for I had decided not to remember her; it was, between the two of us, it was she who had lost more than me. Because how could I lose anything, before I gained it. She never had feelings for me. She lost me, my love. Yes she surly could get it from others, but not the one which I could have given her. I was lost somewhere, I didn't know where, because I was lost between somewhere and everywhere. I really felt sorry for her, so very sorry for her.

"You have made me stronger
By breaking my heart
You ended my life
And made a better one start
You taught me everything
From falling in love
To letting go off a lie
Yes you have made me stronger baby
By saying GOODBYE"

A NEW LIFE

All set for a new life, a night before my departure. It was Saturday night. I was very busy with my packing from tooth brush to hair gel, from trousers to undies; I was damn confused as well as excited for my professional life. How is it going to be, Female boss and colleagues? Somewhere that horny animal in me was taking a re-birth. I didn't forget to update my face book status despite of my heavy packing schedule.

"New life... Bangalore! I am coming ZzzzzZzzzz...."

Twenty four likes and some fifty comment. HohO.. Least expected, as I never cared to post any comment on their stupid status. But yeah I had something in me, Ah!

But my love's lost in the mist of fate. That's the only thing that hurts. And it hurts badly. Never mind, because I still know the way she smells, ANGELIC. Well I want to sing aloud. Feels like a paradox.

At least I am feeling happy, though just a little.

"So?" Dev said with a mysterious expression.

"So what?"

"Party? Beer I mean." he said.

"NO! You know that I don't like all this now."

"Oh! Shut up. It's been ages since the last time we boozed like hell and you are going tomorrow, let's go." Emotional Dev.

"Okay."

Three tuborgs down, later Harsh joined us; you could call it my farewell party. I was surely going to miss these dumb fuckers. They meant a lot to me.

It was quite a mix. Dev with his "being single" stories, Harsh with his "Being committed" and of course me with my "Being broken" stories. As beer was making us high, our sad stories were reaching their peak. Maybe "Being Sad" was the theme of the party. With every possible English, Hindi, Punjabi sad song, we celebrated the night. When your heart is broken and you listen to those sad numbers, you feel like as if they were sung only for you, for that very moment. We boozed and boozed like hell. The butter chickens and Cheese tikkas remained as spectators only. Tuborg was enough for us. With sadness in environment I fell asleep.

Finally, the day arrived. It was Sunday. Harsh and Dev came to see me off, luggage rolled in the cab, we headed for the airport, with every step I was trying to forget everything about her, yes somewhere down the line she was still ruling my heart and mind. For an instance, I thought of calling her, but dropped the idea, as we reached the airport, we were almost on time. I hugged both of them. Yes it was kind of an emotional moment, I entered the airport, with security checkups and other formalities sooner I settled myself in the plane. Before switching off my phone the thought of calling Sneha again struck me, but I didn't.

Oh! Those Air India's hostesses. Damn, two of them were too hot. I tried to fancy my chances with one of them but again it was their duty to talk nicely with passengers that is what they are paid for.

BANGALORE

"I wanna be a billionaire, so freaking bad..."

"Forget billionaire, I'm going to be a gazillionbrazillibrilmillitrilizillionare!!!!!"

My flight landed in Bangalore at around five. For a change it was on time, flights in India are delayed by some random reasons. Anyhow, Finally I was there, Altogether a new picture for me, how was it going to be?

I came out of the airport, I had to find an auto to go to my destination, I fumbled in my pockets to find the slip of paper with my new address, I couldn't find it in my jeans, and almost panicked, I didn't know any place in Bangalore. I opened my wallet and found my address. I heaved a sigh of relief. I came to auto stand, three drivers were arguing with each other over the next passenger.

"Hotel sir, Hotel?" One driver pushed back the other two.

"No Hotel" I said and showed him the address slip.

One thing about Bangalore's auto drivers I liked was that they were educated enough, to read what address it was showing. Well! Quite impressive.

I loaded the luggage, "Meter?" I asked.

He nodded and gave me a mysterious smile, well! I was not sure, what that was.

The first impression of the city was an awesome one, Unlike Delhi, controlled traffic, no mad beggars around. It was the perfect rosy picture; I was carrying in my mind. First time, I literally came across to the place, justifying the hoardings "Keep your city clean and green".

When the cab finally reached the company guest house, my eye popped out as I had the glimpse of meter reading, It was showing Rs 220, Damn, mere 10 miles and the fare was, "What the fuck", Yes, the first three words came in my mind, Anyways I had to pay.

The Gurkha was busy with his crime novel, those thick, cheap Hindi novels with melodramatic endings; probably the hero in this novel had just haunted another victim, raped her, or stolen her kidney or done some bizarre stuff. I say that because I could make it out in his male vent smile.

"Who are you, what do you want?" The Gurkha demanded, his smile long gone, brows shrunk.

"I am Employee of this company."

"Can I see your I-Card?" brows relaxed.

"No, I have appointment letter."

"Okay, Show." As if, he was the boss.

As I handed him my letter, with an x-ray from top to bottom, he told me "Go in, cross the lawn and the reception is right there." I doubt if he could really make out what the letter was all about, except my salary figures.

The place had nothing spectacular in it, "just Okay" the perfect word to categorize it, but literally I had no other option. It was going to be my temporary home in Bangalore, Yes temporary, because I was just allowed to give rest to my ass there for 2 weeks, anyways, not at all a bad option to start up with.

Due to a restless and tired day, I thought of taking a power nap, I was yet to enter my dream world, when some jackass knocked at the door and it was a call for dinner, Dinner at 7? Ah! That was one more disgusting thing for me. But yes, I was hungry too, so accepted the call.

I came out of the room and saw a girl battling with newspaper in the lobby. I checked her out from the corner of my eye, her waist length hair ripped as she tapped the newspaper stand with her fingers like some business corporate checking the elevations and depressions of Sensex. But she didn't seem to be the one. She had perfect features. That is all it takes to make people beautiful, normal body, yet why does nature mess up so many times? Her tiny pink bindi matched her light pink and white salwar kameez and Elegant is the best word to describe her.

Looking at the dining table, at first instance one would imagine a treat for the tummy. Big spoons, small spoons, knives, forks, chopsticks, toothpicks. The first thing came in my mind, "Boohoo... Big spoons - Talumai soup , Chopsticks – Chop Saucy and blah blah "But soon the real scene was a little different one, it started with rice and ended up at dal, yes rice to dal, that's it. Shaaay! No starters, nothing. Wtf?

The forks and knifes were only to look at, they really had no role to play with, more spectators.

Without thinking any more shit, I preferred to hit the food, whatever it was. I was hungry. Later she joined me, the business corporate look alike, elegant beauty. Perhaps we were the only two, there in guest house.

"Hi I am Nikhil" as we exchanged hellos.

"Hello Kritika." She said.

She was least interested in giving a glance at me after the first hello was exchanged. May be she was a strong believer of the saying, "never talk while you eat" But I always had a habit to utter something with every bite. While I was battling to mix the rice with dal, I asked her "Which department?"

"Computers and you?" She said and asked me to pass the rice bowl.

"Mechanical" I said with a proud smile.

Ah! Don't tell me, she liked it, rice and dal. But actually she was or maybe she was so damn hungry or may be something else, as she asked me to pass the dal this time. "Oh! Girl why don't you keep it with you? No! No! Ask the cook to pack it for you so that you can have it tomorrow and day after "Well! Just a thought, off course I didn't say it aloud. But she actually liked it, for me it was all shit in yellow white color.

Pass the dal, pass the rice and nothing. Except the passing she didn't care to say anything. If not hugs and kisses I was expecting a healthy conversation at least. But it was nothing but passing. The sound of onion bit which she was chewing after every spoon of the delicious meal was irritating me. I was done with my food and waited for her, obeying table manners. At last Pheeewwww! She was done... with a tissue passing and with good night greetings she left the place. A real combo of boring stuff and bad food with a beautiful girl it was.

The next day of my life was going to be the one of the important ones; it was the time to see what the professional life is all about? New interesting people or some noobs. It was time to bend down and let the boss screw me in every possible way. The next page will tell you how my professional life kicked off.

PROFESSIONAL KICK!!

Just a word on that, it began with a lot of chaos and flew into rage. Getting started was kind of very hectic job, first waking up at around 7 in morning, the thing which I had never ever done in my life. I could not really sleep a night before, may be the new environment was the reason which was making it uncomfortable for me or maybe I was missing Sneha. So many random thoughts kept on hitting my mind all night long. In patches, I just managed to sleep for 3 hours and 20 minutes. I was excited but nervous. I was happy but not delighted.

I woke up around 7, took a bath. Black trousers, pink shirt and black shoes. That was me. While I was tying the tie in front of mirror, I could see the nervous Nikhil standing tall. College life, cafeteria, Sneha, love, lust and all were the part of past and I was going to take a step forward.

Finally with all these thoughts I reached the company head office. Courtesy: Company pick and drop cab. Welcome to a world, where people talk about each other and everyone lies and tries to be something. I entered the place, met the lady at the reception, She made a call, talked with some body and escorted me to a room. I went in; a nerdy old man sat on a revolving chair. He glanced at me from head to toe, with his fingers constantly tapping the table.

"Can I see your file" He said. I handed him my file and stood quietly in front of him. My hands were sweating as he glanced at my certificates. He kept on checking them for almost 10 minutes and I was just looking around, waiting, because it was not less than hell. Finally he was done with no real expressions.

"Okay Nikhil, you are going to work under me." Stretching his hands over the table.

"My pleasure sir." I smiled at him.

"But you have to work really hard. I have seen your mark sheets and this company has very high reputation." His fat face lit up and he closed his eyes.

"Sure sir."

He gave me a bunch of project files and asked me to go through them.

It's bad when you hate your job in the first hour of the first day of office. While I was checking those flies, I tried my level best to see if I could make out what exactly they were all about. But everything was going over my head except some words like machines tools graphs etc. They say "Bookish knowledge is not enough, you need to have practical knowledge too." But in my case even bookish knowledge was no way adequate. I somehow managed to clear my exams. But practical stuff! I could count on my fingers how many practical classes I had attended in my whole engineering course. Yes, if they could have asked me about the girls, I would have done wonders. But unfortunately I was being hired in a mechanics department.

Coffee break, Lunch break, shuffling the files and nothing! I had nothing to do but yeah a lot to do. Nothing because I had no clue what those files were all about. All because, I had to do that work, or my boss would kick my ass.

I tried my level best to check what was there in those files, but my mind was all blank. I checked the time, it was 3. I knew anytime, the bald headed boss could call me and as I was thinking, I got a call. Oh! Seriously what timing? As I went in he was busy with some file stuff. He looked at me with no expressions and asked me "Nikhil are you done?"

"Yes sir, almost. In an hour or two I will." I lied to him.

"Good but no need to do that, you have been shifted to Machines department and you are going to work under Mr. Mridul Sharma as a trainee."

OH MYGOD! I heaved a sigh of relief. My! My! That meant I was not going to face that nerdy, bald headed, dumbass any more.

Oh! No more files. Oh! May be they had realized that a talent like mine shouldn't not be wasted in file handling stuff. Whatever the reason might be, I was saved from getting screwed by that nerd. Now the question was who is Mridul Sharma? I was just hoping for something good to happen now.

I came out with a sigh of relief. Phew! Okay Nick time to see what's next.

I looked up at the huge board that had all the details about the building.

"Machines, 3rd floor." I tried to memorize.

The building was newly built and well maintained. One could spot the new electronic gadgets at every other step, CCTV cameras, and Electronic boards. The lift though was a complicated one. Different lifts stopped at different floors. So it took me some time to get used to it.

I jumped alternate stairs to reach the third floor.

Starting from left to right. Oiling. Tools. Machines lab. Machines Department. It was Machines department in the right corner. I took a deep breath and went in. Damn, it was altogether a different scene, there were around five guys inside, and two of them were busy discussing their weekend party. A guy in the corner was doing something on his laptop, maybe he was searching the new release of Naughty America, from the corner of my eyes I could see a girl lying sideways on the screen in red and blue. The other two were discussing some project work. Oh! May be the studious brats of the lot. None of them really cared to give a glance at me; everyone was busy with his or her respective irrelevant and relevant work. I stood there for two minutes and someone called me. "Hey out."

A guy with long hair, well built, funky style, goatee, pierced ears, white shirt, blue jeans. Oh! I thought he was one more trainee around like me.

"Hi! Do you know where Mr. Mridul Sharma is?"

"Well! That's me, tell me."

Oh! The guy under whom I was going to work was kind of cool, unlike, the conventional suited booted bosses. Destiny. May be it was my luck, that took me there and saved me from getting screwed by that bald headed nerdy boss. But it was just his appearance; the real part of him was yet a mystery for me.

"Hello sir, I am Nikhil."

"Oh! Nikhil Arora, New joinee, Mr. Mishra informed me about you."

"Oh!" I smiled at him.

"I am Mridul, call me Mridul. Don't call me 'sir', I joined last year."

"Fine, Mridul."

"So have you liked the company so far or not." With the last word, he took his seat on big round revolving chair.

"Can't say, I just joined some six hours back. Well! Session with Mr. Mishra went well."

I made a diplomatic statement with a spice of lie. Ah! Good session? Damn! It had been a pathetic one.

"Oh! Really? I can't believe this."

"What?"

"Yes! How can you like checking his age old files?"

"Yes, that part was a little boring."

"Now you are telling me the truth." He winked at me.

The ice between us broke the very next second and probably by that time it had submitted to the sun, facilitating the fusion reaction there and lightening up my life. The first day ended up with some elevations and depressions and then an elevation. I was bored, tired, lost, and lost in the thoughts of Sneha. All the things we used to do. I had moved on, but somewhere Sneha was still there in my mind with an image fading day by day. I was carrying an image of"Bad Boy" before I met her. I was a person with no deep perception of life who only lived for his own satisfaction and had little or no empathy for other people. Somebody who knew that he was a bad boy, who he was on the wrong path but still never bothered to change for the better. But she changed me, she made me study, although the reason was different one but she always stood next to me. Those exams. Those interviews. Failures. Success. Rejection. Everywhere, except the last time we met, perhaps the most important one. I was all alone with good and bad memories.

A NEW CHAPTER IN LIFE

She came to me, I was lost in my thoughts, and I was clueless. She explored my body, licked, swallowed and then left and I was kind of hurt, fucking culicidae, female mosquito, not sure if that was her, but a wild guess.

"Hey!" I heard a sweet voice in the lobby area and it was Kritika the lady in love with rice and dal.

"Hi." I said.

"So how are you doing?" She said.

"Well good."

Oh! She was not dumb, she could speak. That was a surprise for me, I did not expect her to take the initiative and talk to me at least after the dinner table encounter. I had thought image of her as a girl with attitude who just loved unhealthy tasteless food. But I was kind of wrong, we chatted a lot that day. She told me, she was from Mumbai, Oh! Political views. Discussions. Boring stuff. If some other day you would ask me to discuss those topics, I would surely make faces. But on that day it was good, at least it was helping us to kill time. Ah! Who doesn't enjoy the company of a beautiful girl?

After dinner we went for a walk, we were kind of getting friendly with each other. The ice was certainly breaking between us but on the slower side. She was hot, beautiful, interesting too. The whole package was good, if you ignore her choice of food.

"Hey what's up man?" Mridul turned his head towards me while checking some files.

"Nothing, you say?"

Working under Mridul was more of fun. Unlike the conventional bosses he was different. In less than a week we were more of friends rather than sharing a typical boss - trainee relationship. He had made things simpler and quite comfortable for me. He was the same with others too but I could feel the leniency from his side towards me in the first week only because I had done almost nothing in those four and half days. May be he had a soft corner for a guy who was from his city, as Mridul was also from Delhi. It was the last working day, Friday, end of the first week of professional life. If I had to summarize the first week's happenings, I would say, it was all good. Better then my expectations. In fact one of the better things that had happened to me since Sneha left me. In addition to that, my bond with Kritika had grown the coming. We had planned an outing too on the coming weekend, an unofficial date.

"So any plans for weekend?" He said.

"Not really, going out with a friend may be."

"Oh! Friend.... Girl friend?" Mridul winked at me.

"No girl friend, just a five days old friend, met her in the guest house."

"Guest house? So you are staying there?"

"Yes."

"Oh! But I believe they won't allow you to stay there for more than a week, so did you start your search for new home?"

"No. Kept it for the weekend."

"Okay. If you don't mind you can join me, I stay alone, I too need a roommate."

I desperately needed a place to stay. Nobody was a better choice than Mridul. "I was not a fool to say no to him. "In an instant I said yes to him.

"Okay perfect, So Sunday? Move in on Sunday morning, as I would be busy tomorrow, you know girlfriend and all."

"Okay fine."

I needed a roommate seriously because the minute I stepped out of office, I was haunted by the thoughts of Sneha, though I had Kritika with me to talk to whenever I was low but Sneha never left my mind. The way she used to talk, walk and everything. Mridul was a dude who always carried an attitude of I don't give a damn. He was more like me, or may be the way I was, before I met Sneha. So he was the perfect option for me to find my lost identity and to get over Sneha.

UNOFFICIAL DATE

Popcorn – Cold drink, the ideal combo to kill time, when you accidentally find yourself stuck in a movie, which is kind of far away from your interest or to be precise a boring one. That is what I was doing. Three large packs were already jumping in my stomach, but the movie was not ready to end. I don't know why but Kritika was finding it very interesting. But I was not surprised by it. The dining table experience with her, the affection she showed towards dal and rice, all pointed to that. We were poles apart but we were kind of friends. Maybe, we guys had no other option. Yes she was hot and sexy, with an awesome dressing sense, which I liked the most. But that was my reason of hanging out with her. But I really couldn't make out why she was showing interest in an ugly brat like me, though not that ugly.

And finally, the director decided to make it end, Mercy!!

Phewwww... It was over, literally a torture.

As we came out, I said..

"Did I tell you, I am leaving the guest house tomorrow?"

"What? Why?"

"Huh! I got a roommate and none other than my boss."

"Oh! That's cool, but you should have told me earlier."

"I am telling you, I am leaving tomorrow not today."

"Lucky you, I still have to start my search."

"Don't worry, we will find one for you too."

"We?" and she made 'that' face.

"Yes, me and you."

"Oh! Yes." And she made 'that' face again with hesitation this time.

I had not much to carry with me, just two suitcases and a teddy which Sneha had gifted me on my B'day. It was kind of girly stuff, but I used to sleep with the teddy remembering Sneha, my first love although a complicated one.

I picked my stuff and met Kritika. We shared good bye greetings, But she seemed to be a little on the sadder side, as she was going to stay alone, no more walks. I gave her a side hug, tapped my hand on her head and told her, "Don't worry, we will find a home for you soon." And she gave me a million dollar smile; we almost shared the unsaid feelings that we were friends now and had to cover a lot of distance.

CHANGE AGAIN!!

Finally, I was there in my new home in Bangalore. Hopefully the permanent one, fingers crossed. Mridul was in the kitchen by the time I reached the place. He was preparing some lemon water. Courtesy: Last night's heavy boozing with screwing resulting into a bad hangover. The place was all messed up; it had two bedrooms, one hall and a small, currently in ugliest possible appearance kitchen. One corner of the hall had a number of bottles of different brands of whiskey and beer. Seriously he was a big time boozer. There were some condoms too lying on the center table. There is a small story related to this stuff, the first time one of our friend was going for a date we all went to buy a condom for him, none dared to ask the medical guy for condom .We came back and cancelled the date. Later we discovered that AIDS control society is coming up with the condom with name "That"...as most of us go to shop and say. Another was DIPPER as behind all trucks it is written use dipper at night. I could see myself going one year back to the life I used to live. The reason I decided to go with Mridul's offer was to find my lost identity and to get out of that image of being a broken hearted lover. Mridul asked me to keep my luggage in his room despite of the fact that it was a two bed room set and I asked him about this. He informed me the other room was for fun time aka screwing room, as he winked at me. Oh!

I spent the next few hours in unpacking my stuff and arranging them in the almirah, Phew! That was the only thing which I did not have to share, while Mridul was lying on the bed, watching me. Finally when I announced that I was done with arranging and stuffing the things, Mridul stood up and came up with ground rules of the flat.

"Coming late is not a problem, coming with a female friend is not at all a problem, but taking her to the master bed room is a problem, until or unless she holds the tag of girl friend. Drinking, smoking is all allowed, but not in the master bedroom, let's don't make our living place dirty. Electric bill, water bill and all other fucking bills will be shared. "

"And last but not the least, here no one is boss or no one is trainee, just roommates or can call Delhi heights surviving in Mallus." Finally he took a deep breath phewwwwwww....

Fuck! Literally a big fuck, but full of pleasure, the kind of feeling one gets, I got the same feeling, satisfied, happy inside. I could feel the fresh breath of life, which I used to experience before I met Sneha.

"Do you read horoscopes?" He asked

"No. Do you believe in them?"

"Yes and no." He said

"What do you mean by yes and no?"

"See whatever these astrologers write, things happen exactly contrary to that. For example : Today it said, A lonely day ahead, No friends will find time for you, but see what happened, you are here. I have a friend with whom I am going to fuck my whole day, lets party, drink like fish, eat like pig, swing in different women every night and life will be one grand mad bash."

I was unable to utter anything, I was just happy, emotionless with hell lot of emotions rising and falling in me, I could see myself regaining my lost identity from the distance but there was one problem and a fucking big one, I had promised Kritika that I will join her in her new home search.

"Great but ..." and I was clueless.

"But what?"

"I have to go somewhere else."

"Where? Girlfriend? But as far as I know you don't have any."

"Yes, but a friend, I have to go with her in search of a flat."

"Oh! But what if I solve your problem?"

"What? Really? How?" I sounded excited.

"Calm down Nick, so many questions."

"Okay! Okay... Tell me." Excitation at its peak.

"First tell me, if she is hot. I mean not like those aunty types, you know what I mean."

Grrrrr.... Why he was asking that? Mridul's image in my mind was gradually emerging as a horny animal, but what was cooking in his mind? Solving my problem - Asking if she is hot? I had no clue.

"What? Anyways, yeah she is kind of hot."

"Okay done, Problem solved."

"What? What are you talking about?" Almost scratching my head.

He was throwing his mischievous words at me and I was like... Then he was like... then we were like... And ended up with "What?"

"Ah! If your friend has no problem, she can move in with Natasha, my girl friend."

"And I bet ya, she won't be having any problem. Natasha is super cool." He added.

Super cool - Air conditioner? Some talcum powder? I could never understand the real definition of being cool. I remember some jerks in college, with pierced ears, brows, tongue. God know if they had pierced dicks too, Tattoos all over and defining themselves cool. For me they were, nothing less than ugly brats. So Natasha was that type?

Looking at Mridul, I could expect that too or she was cool in some other sense like cool headed. Well! Still a mystery. But I was kind of least bothered by that neither I had to date her nor I was going to stay with her. We all planned to meet at Brigade road the same evening.

FUN AND MYSTERY

Green. Red. Orange. Green. After passing some 10 traffic signals we finally reached there, Brigade road. Natasha the cool and Kritika the elegant were supposed to join us later. Scene at Brigade road in the evening was full of young people or rather I should say young lovers. One could see all the poor couples who were dying to eat their partners, kissing in different corners in the dark in the shed of the parking, somewhere anywhere. Poor I say because they didn't even have enough money to afford a room where they can do those acrobatic moves in privacy. There are many people who are keen to disturb these young lovers. These are police constables like ticket checkers, their family also survive on bribe. In exchange of few hundred bucks they allow them to continue their public affection. Then there are bunch of teenagers who sit around these couples or settle themselves in such a way that they can glance at the show. For them it's like watching a porn movie and that too free of cost.

When the testosterone runs high, you don't see any distraction only attraction. May be that is why this place is still a favorite with these sexually desperate and frustrated couples. I calculated quickly in my mind. If I open a room service out here, it will make me a fortune. I can charge thousand rupees an hour or more for renting out a room to those morons.

Later Natsha and Kritika joined us. The moment Kritika came up to the scene, Mridul whispered in my ear, "Fuck how you can call her kind of hot, Man she is super hot." Kritika was wearing a skinny pair of jeans and her red tee was enhanced her red hot frame. On the other hand, I found Natasha kind of cool, kind of hot, not elegant, bitchy she had pierced brows it was actually going with her outlook. In short, I liked her. But my like and dislike was not really required, we were there to see if Kritika could settle with Natasha or vice versa.

It was all quiet, Natasha and Mridul in the front and me and Kritika on the back seat. Was that a silence before a disaster? Actually No. Mridul and I tried to break the silence but it didn't work. Girls were lost in their own world. Natasha had a kind of gf-bf fight with Mridul so she was trying to show her anger by remaining Shhshhh... And Kritika Ah! Definitely she was shy, lil introvert, she took some time to get along. Once got on, She was great to hang around with, in our one week old friendship I had gathered that fact about her. Thankfully Mridul was playing some good Punjabi numbers, though not loud but anytime, I like those beats. Those Punjabi beats covered Mridul's poor jokes, which he was throwing every next minute, trying his best to make the environment a rocking one. But it was not working. Ending up with some hmmmmss and a rare laugh especially by me, complimenting my boss aka roommate.

"You know what Nick? I guess the fucking astrologer was right."

"What? Which one?"

"That one man... Lonely day without friends."

"Yes I do have so called friends with me, but as mere spectators." He added.

"Hahaha! Anyways, where are we going?"

"Can you really see us going somewhere?"

"Nooo..." Looking around.

Actually it was the 7th time, no... no... 8th time that we were passing the same path, one corner to the other corner, 180 degree move and 360 degree turn around and then straight 180 degree. Loop continues. Passing roadside young poor lovers.

"Idiot this is Brigade's road and people out here come for two things only."

"And what are they?"

"First, When they feel like eating their partner's different body parts courtesy dark empty spaces around the corner and second, to roam around on smooth 4 Km track with beer and partner or friends to have fun or for making fun of those roadside lovers."

"Okay, interesting."

"Fuck interesting. Right now I feel like hitting my head on steering."

"Go ahead baby, don't feel... Just do it "Natasha said checking the CD cover.

It was the first time Natasha uttered a full six words sentence since she came on the scene, else it was me and Mridul only who were trying to kill the silence. Talking about Kritika she was all Shhhhh... least interested in uttering even a word, as if they are going to charge her some bucks per word like prepaid account.

"You know what guys? "Mridul shouted.

"Once Martin Luther king said: If you cannot run, at least walk, if you cannot walk, at least drag, if u cannot drag, at least pretend to move."

Santa was listening to it quite amused and asked,

"Sir, where are we going?"

Finally he succeeded in breaking the silence, we all laughed out loudly. For an instance, one might wonder, what the equation between Martin Luther king and Santa is, but yeah lets all say hail Santa, his stupidity entertained us.

"Okay 10 rounds over. Ice cream guys?" Mridul asked.

"Thank god, you finally realized we need something to eat too." Natasha again commented.

Well! Natasha was one of the funny characters around. It's always good to see someone kicking your boss's ass with words so I was enjoying that. Mridul and I stepped out and went to catch all the different flavors of ice creams symbolizing our different tastes or may be nature too, but for the time being we were accompanying each other as we came back with cups of strawberry, vanilla and other flavors. The scene in the car was all changed in just 10 minutes. Natasha had shifted to driving seat while Kritika was on the front seat. Both were discussing, talking about fashion, wardrobe collection, and blah blah. Girlish talks. It was amazing, how everything turned around in just 10 minutes. It just justified the statement "Expect unexpected from beautiful girls" whatever it was, but it suddenly made everything so cheerful, Actually Natasha and Kritika liked each other which was the most important thing. Kritika told me "She can shift to Natasha's flat tomorrow". Me and Mridul were just surprised and numb, wondering how it had happened. It had appeared an impossible task some 20 minutes back. Seriously even today we guys wonder what had happened in those 10 minutes. But for me that evening had revived the hopes of "being happy "again. I actually liked every bit of the moment. I was just wondering if it could work to get me out of the state heart break. I desperately needed some companions to talk to and see they were right there. I had my group.

LEARNING TO UNDERSTAND

I want to shout, throw my soul out. Scare you, the all knowing god. I want to shout, shout away all my joy, breathe away all my pain, exhale and just express myself. I cannot hold it inside myself any longer, trapped within my heart, hidden underneath my throat. I need to shout, right now, shout, shout out loud, loud just enough. Dissipating all my agony, this anger. I want to break the very wall I lean on, not caring consequences, hit it so hard, even if the bones in my tiny, tiny fist are crushed and powdered. SHOUT OUT! HIT THE WALL! Just break free and go berserk! Letting go of the beast within, coming out, shouting out loudly my voice is breaking, doesn't matter just breathing against it. Just break free. Now do you feel my anger dear god? Feel it?

There was once a man who went to see a mystic who was reputed to be very knowledgeable.

"Sir," he said. "I lead a comfortable life and have no desire for anything material in nature and yet I always feel as though my life is missing something. I would like nothing more than just to be happy."

The mystic replied, "I have the answer that will solve your problem but it entails some work on your part." The man readily agreed and begged him to go on.

"Go and travel the world and look for the happiest man in the world and when you find him, ask him for his shirt and put it on."

The seeker immediately set out looking for happy people. One by one he came across various individuals, each one naming another happier than themselves.

After many months of travelling from one country to another, he found out that the happiest man in the world lived somewhere in the woods near a village in India. When he reached the place, he followed the echoes of laughter he heard among the trees. Finally coming face to face with an old man, he asked him, "Are you the happiest man in the world?"

"Yes, I Am." replied the old man.

The seeker met him and relayed to him the purpose of his search and then asked, "I have been ordered by a great mystic to wear your shirt; please give it to me and I will give you anything you ask for in exchange."

The happiest man looked at him closely and burst into uncontrollable fits of laughter. He laughed and laughed and he laughed much to the annoyance of the seeker. "Are you insane that you laugh at such a serious request?"Asked the seeker.

"Maybe," replied the happiest man. "But if you had taken the trouble to look, you will see that I am not wearing a shirt."

"What do I do now?" Sighed the seeker, feeling tired and dejected.

"Don't worry," consoled the happiest man, "you will now be able to fulfill your quest. When you strive for something unattainable, the very effort you put in is the exercise that you need to achieve what is needed. When a man gathers all his strength to jump across a stream as though it was wider than it is, he gets across."

The happiest man then took off his turban, a part of which had concealed his face. The seeker then saw that he was none other than the original mystic who had given him the advice.

"But why did you not tell me this when I first came to see you?"The seeker asked, completely confused.

"Because you were not ready then. You needed to go through the effort and the experience which would help you develop the capacity to understand."

And I know that your grandfather told you things.

I can see myself like the restless ocean, finding a little peace here and there, but nothing permanent enough to satisfy me. So the pursuit continues...the desire to find this secret spring is one of the most powerful fuels that drives humanity. Like searching for it in many places – in relationships, careers, going to the movies, consuming alcohol. Buying clothes, etc. These are basically the things that lie outside me, implying that happiness is thought to be found through the outside world.

Yet, within myself I can feel that there is more to happiness than the pursuit of pleasures and possessions. I have a mysterious feeling that this spring of happiness exists somewhere and that makes life worthwhile. I keep on telling myself that somehow, somewhere, I may stumble onto its secret. Sometimes I feel that I have found it – only to find it deceptive, leaving me disillusioned and unhappy.

But now, I have decided not to waste my tears and pretend to be happy, at least happiness might come and knock on my door. This new life has bought me so much and made me feel so happy. Made me realize many more things. I feel now is the right time to go with the flow and broaden my smile rather than cry for all that had happened to me in the past. At least I can try, I don't know... But I will...

STRUGGLING TO FIND MY WAY

Touch it gently put two fingers inside, if its wide use three fingers make sure it's wet and rub up and down, yeah that's how you wash a cup. Professional life plus living on my own was teaching me so many things. New experiences and household work was part of it. Though I did not really love it but we guys had no other option. Finding a servant in Bangalore is a real big time job, one can easily get those normal servants who can satisfy your normal household things but who could tolerate and bear the weird life we alcoholics and freaks was yet to be looked for. In the last two months my life had changed and the process was still on bed. At every other step, something new was waiting for me. Work - Whiskey - Beer - Party - Weekend – Kritika- Mridul - Natasha, they were the basic ingredients of bringing back the spice in my life. I was happy and cheerful again.

Priorities were changing rapidly, focus was more on career. All focus was on my own knowledge. It was difficult to know everything inside out but I wanted to know and for all this, I would give credit to Mridul, he was behaving like a perfect roommate, rather a real time big brother. The best thing in him was that he was good in managing things the way he used to do his work with sincerity for five days and during the weekend he was altogether a different guy, from HR professional to spoiled, horny animal, alcoholic freak. He was perfect in switching gears of life and my make over was still going on. I was not happy because it was all perfect rather I started looking beyond imperfection. I started believing that I could not change my destiny but I could surely learn to live with whatever came to me.

I was a prince living in a glass house. When one day someone threw a stone... another and then another and suddenly it cracked. I tried to save my glass house but out of nowhere within seconds it came crashing down. It shattered right before my eyes. I just couldn't stop it from tumbling down. It kept falling apart from time to time but I had successfully restored it. Yet still one day it crashed and all the broken pieces shattered. I tried picking them up bleeding in the process... trying to clear the clutter I had made... the tears just kept flowing never to stop... they overflowed and washed away the small pieces of glass that had fallen ... but somehow the pieces that had embedded into my soul as I had gathered them... the pieces that had scarred me for life were still there... deeply embedded... I tried to scrape them, but somehow got lost. How was I?

To know that these wounds would bleed yet again after so long… but they do… and they bleed with so much of agonizing pain that I can feel it as if it were yesterday.

I cried today. Why I have no idea. Maybe it was my anger. All vented up and bottled inside me. But I cried… to my hearts fullest … I cried, I let out my tears… after so long. Why? Why did I suddenly break down? Why did I suddenly lose it? I wonder if there is something I am missing in my life? Or is it just that these days I am pleading Insanity!

I am getting sane... yes I think it's about time I did talk sense. Thinking of what I wrote last night. I just couldn't rest. I kept pondering over and over and yet over again. Suddenly life seemed to flash back… zipity zap! And boom I was back where I had started… did I just lose a piece of me in this insane world of freaks. But I believe I am not the average human anyways, I am so aslant and confused at times, not too much but I do. Like I did at my own piece after I got the job.

Here I stand head up high wishing for all of this to end. I want a battle I seek truce or fight to death!! I guess I needed to find that out since I had people worrying about my life.

I was a different man when I woke up this morning. I could feel nothing; I had never felt like this before. I was free! I've stopped being nice and I've decided not to compromise anymore. Why should

I be giving in when no one else does? Just to keep things moving? How important is that when you are of no importance? Today I'll walk, talk, act do whatever I like... with no strings attached.

GOING AHEAD, taking chances, telling the truth, dating someone totally wrong for me, saying no, spending all my cash, getting to know someone at random, No more love, singing out loudly, laughing my ass out, laughing at a stupid joke, telling someone how much they meant for me, Telling a jerk what I think about him, laughing until my stomach hurts, In short I had learned to live again with no regrets.

Kritika and I were now kind of best friends. Mridul was kind of big brother and Natasha was weird but still we were kind of friends. But my mind was still stuck in Sneha, though the intensity was very low. But they have said rightly, "It is really a big time job, to forget people whom you love."

Sometimes I think, she must be at a better place, but I wish if I could see her face again. Oh! I know you are where you need to be, even though it's not right here with me, remembering Sneha always bring a smile on my face. Kritika was the one who brightens up very possible situation with her affection and care towards me. It was perfect still imperfect and I was happy.

My first love was nothing less than a nightmare for me. But I fought hard to be what I was, after a bad period of love life....I am back and I am back with a big bang...with lots of energy actually boost is the secret of my energy. Boost of boozing and new friends. Boost of new flavor of life.

Darn! Weekdays, Job, Office, Weekdays were like.

Monday- Ughh its Monday.

Tuesday- Well at least its Tuesday.

Wednesday- Wow, it's already Wednesday.

Thursday- Hey, tomorrow's Friday!

Friday- Yes Weekend!

Saturday- -PARTY- Boozing - Dead - Fucking.

Sunday- CRAP tomorrow's MONDAY. But party is still on.

Wouldn't life be easier if sweat pants were sexy, junk food didn't make you fat, Monday mornings were fun and love never hurt? Great thought, but still not a real one, a stupid one.

Only two things are infinite:

* Universe

* Human Stupidity

- Elbert Einstein.

Well now if you are not a tube light, which takes around 10 seconds and still struggles to light up my room, you must have gathered the reason behind my voyage.

NATASHA'S B'DAY PARTY

Venue: our two room flat.

Me, Mridul, Kritika, Natasha and full on drama.

I was like...... She was like....... He was like......Okay, We were like.... "Okay, Okay! Listen to me, Stay" Mridul followed Natasha, as she headed towards the room with red face, hot steaming brain, angry. They went in and shut the door. I could hear some arguments going on in the closed room. Oh! One more fight, the more they love each other, the more they fight. Is this the way to show their love for each other? If so, I would never go for it. I was least bothered with their act, actually, all those acts of these weird lovers used to spoil my mood, just like the party was on the verge of being spoiled before it could even start. But like always, something unexpected was coming on my way. I was thinking now I could open my first bottle of beer, but literally was in no mood to drink, suddenly I felt someone calling my name and, "oh baby! I am thirsty for the touch of your lips, come hit me, eat me, bite me."

I heard it many times, I felt, it was coming from somewhere in the fridge, I opened the fridge, bottle jumped out of the fridge, hugged me, took its cap off and said, Kiss me honey.. Kiss me...

The intensity of arguments between Mridul and Natasha was low by now there was no real screaming, which could disturb my love making with tuborg. But they were both in the room still, may be that screaming had changed to moaning by now. Kritika was still busy on the phone, for the last 30 minutes, God knows to whom she was talking?

Well! I liked the beer, it's always good to enjoy it alone, for saying it was a party, a birthday party. But it was only me, who actually had the taste of party, others were busy fighting, screaming, whispering or moaning. Two beers down, and still there was no sign of those 3 idiots, Mridul and Natasha were still locked in the room, yes! Kritika had changed her position from lobby area to balcony, but was still busy with that stupid phone, and me? Oh! I was enjoying the moment and again I kissed the lips of the bottle tough, after 2 down, the kissing was no more a passionate one but still you can call it smooth love making. But every time I used to drink, I used to miss Sneha, she would come and hit the memories like a hammer, like putting salt on my wounds and I could feel the pain all over again. I used to hold myself back but sometimes, I used to fail and drops of tears would kiss my cheeks. No one to talk to: All were busy in their stupid acts. I found myself drowning in her memories all over again, Sneha this.... Sneha that.... Sneha met... Sneha what .... Sneha left.....

I was so lost in Sneha's thoughts, that for a second, I couldn't realize that Kritika was done with her call and was sitting next to me. Silent and lost.

"So what's up girl?" I asked, trying to hide my emotions.

"Nothing." She said

I could feel that there was something wrong, But what was that? I had never seen her like this, So silent, lost, I could sense, there was something fishy, although I was almost high, but still I was in my senses so that I could see, if my bestie was alright or not...

"What happened?" I asked her.

"Nothing." Looking down at the floor.

"Tell me. What happened?" I asked her

"I said nothing, didn't you hear?" She shouted at me.

"Whom did you call?"

"No one."

"WTF? Tell me."

"Why do you want to know?"

"Because I am your so called bestie."

"Okay, my ex called me."

"Oh! Then?"

"Then what? Arguments..!! He was drunk!!"

"Then? Why are you so silent?" A dumb question from me.

"Oh! Nick, Will you please, shut the fuck up." and she stood up walking rather running towards the balcony.

REAL FEMALE DICTIONARY:

Nothing, forget it = you better figure out what you screwed up.

I am okay = I am not fucking okay.

i don't give a fuck anymore = I still care, but I am tired of arguing.

eye roll = boy you have done it this time get your ass out of there and buy some flowers.

Whatever = your argument is stupid.

I am cold = give me your jacket ASAP.

Leave me alone = get out of here before I slap you.

I love you = tell me you do more.

I followed her and stood next to her, I could really feel she was upset... but why? I had no clue...

"Are you crying?"

"No, I am not, please leave me alone." She squeaked and sniffed.

"Yes... you are!! Tell me what happened?"

"Nothing yaar, he was drunk and started blaming me for all the things that went wrong between us. You know what??? I hate him!! All men are dogs!! I loved him!! He ditched me and still he is blaming me for the break up!! Whooh!!" Kritika had again dipped into one of her hyper paranoid motor mouthing sessions.

It's really a horrible feeling when you see one of your closest friends crying for a boy and all you want to do is go and kill that fucking asshole. Seriously, how could he ditch a girl, whom he loved, or is boy friend girl friend relation is all about lust?

On one side, it was me, who loved a girl, but she didn't. On the other side, it was she, who loved a guy, but he didn't. Both of us were sad, but maybe that was our destiny, heartbroken besties. But it was the first time, when she told me about her boyfriend and all, before that I used to think what a perfect life she must be living. But someone has truly said, "Nothing/nobody is perfect in life." and there it was.

I went close to her and wiped her tears, gave her a smile wrapped my arms round her neck and hugged her. I was sad. She was sad and a hug can do wonders for you to bring out your hidden emotions, I don't know why I hugged her. I don't know why she hugged me. But we were in each other arms, I could feel her breath, I could feel her heart crying and screaming for the stupid guy, who never gave importance to her love and maybe she could feel the same. Maybe, it was the second (the first one was with Sneha) time, that I hugged a girl, without having intentions to measure her bra strap, in short it was all pure, two friends, trying to hold the emotions and transferring the strength to each other. We kept on hugging for some time. I was feeling better now and maybe she was feeling the same way. I never knew a hug could do such wonders for me. We came so close to each other and time had stopped. While I was holding Kritika, I closed my eyes and for an instance, it turned all dark, then after few seconds I could see Sneha, right there, standing right in front of me, looking as beautiful as ever, smiling, She seemed to be happy, I could see myself, still on my knees holding the rose, though the fragrance and freshness of the flower was no longer there. She was wearing the same pink saree, perfect dimples were pressed under high cheeks. But just like that day, she was not with me. I was all alone. I could see myself crying and screaming for her love. I could see Harsh and Dev, somewhere in the corner, don't know what they were doing, maybe they were trying to hold me and boost me up. Everything was flashing upside down, Mom. Dad. Sneha. Dev. Bangalore. Mridul. Kritika. The moment I saw Kritika I don't know what happened, I trembled and opened my eyes, and got myself to reality, Kritika kissed me on my forehead and smiled at me, I didn't know how to react, I was numb, maybe she wanted me to smile back, I tried but couldn't. She tightened her grip round my waist, so did I. She looked into my eyes, so did I. I wanted to run away, but couldn't. She was melting in my arms, came closer to me and more. Like we had said a lot to each other, without uttering a single word. I was losing myself in her, while we were lost in our world, I heard, Mridul screaming...

"Nick!! Man..!! Where the hell are you?"

I went in, holding her hand, holding my emotions, and asked him, "What happened? Why are you shouting?"

"Oh I see," he said with raised eyebrows, looking at me, holding

Kritika's hand.

She threw my hand away and ran away towards the kitchen area hurriedly. I didn't know what had happened to her, maybe she was feeling shy, I could see, she was kind of nervous as she was trying to hide her face. But I could feel the satisfaction in me, as finally I made her smile.

"What's the scene?" Mridul, as he opened the bottle of beer with a tuck.

"Nothing you tell me, What had happened? Why were you guys fighting and where is Natasha?"

"She was feeling little exhausted. So she went off to sleep and Ah! Fight, don't ask me, I am stupid, and I proved it today."

"Exhausted? I see, and what are you talking about? Stupid?"

"Yes."

"I would appreciate, if you can elaborate."

"Actually, we had planned to celebrate her B'day in a grand style with a spice of horniness."

"Oh! Then?"

"Then what? She seemed to be little upset and low, kind of pissed off of some fucking reason."

"Okay, then?"

"I don't know what made me, ask her such an awkward question? She could be on her periods, ignoring all other possibilities which might have been the reason of she being upset."

"Then what?"

"When a girl is pissed off at you, never, under any circumstances, ever say... 'Jeez are you on your period or something ' Because if she is, boy... you are dead. Now don't you dare to ask me THEN?"

"Okay, but this proves you are fucking funny."

OFFICE PRESENTATION

I honestly thought he was going to rap me, he had the craziest look in his eyes and at one point of time he said, "Let's get it on."

"I seriously feel like giving a hard kick on his ass." Mridul said with a crazy look in his eyes as he came in banging the door...

"What?" I said.

I could see a potential rapist right in front of me, "Mr. Mridul Sharma."

"Yes, My dear. There is a breaking news for all of you."

"What? - What? - What? What?"

A scene from some typical Hindi melodrama, all of us looked at Mridul.

"Yes, I just had a meeting with Mr. Saini the head of department;

he asked me to prepare a presentation of the current project and guys it's not only me, it about our team." Mridul said with his hand on his forehead.

"Damn." - "What?" - "Seriously?" - "Fuck!"

We reacted strongly to the fucking news Mridul had given us.

"And guys, it should be done in two days."

There was silence as if someone had died. Presentation and that too in just two days. We all knew it was kind of an impossible task. And if you talk about our team in last three months, our team had not delivered any quality work. No projects. So now was the time, when we had to pay for it. I went almost blank. What to do? In fact not only, all five of us.

Gathering the project files, gathering the information. In fact there were some people who didn't even know what the project was all about and I was one of them. I bet ya, Mridul must be regretting the freedom he had given to all of us. Before this, even I had never given a thought to the fact that we were now the employee of a company and supposed to do our respective work rather than discussing the new releases of naughty America or checking on the girls of the computer's department.

"Okay, I am going to Cat-lab for drawings." Mridul said and asked me to go through some 10 project files.

My second encounter with the project files was no different from the first one. I kept on turning the pages but just couldn't make out what they were all about. The machines layout was an interesting thing to look at. In the last three months it was the only topic which could grab my interest. But now it was not about my interest, nobody was going to give a fuck to my interest, I had to do it or pack my bags and fly back to Delhi. Of course I was in no mood to quit such a happening life which I was leading in Bangalore. So finally, I decided to battle with machines and get the fuck out of them.

After reading some forty pages, I started grabbing something in them, if not more, I could make out the working of cylinders, but that too theoretically, Practical work was still an alien thing for me. For the time being, grabbing the theoretical stuff was more important. It's like when you don't know much about the work either you find every next line important and interesting or you find everything irrelevant and boring. For the initial part, I found everything irrelevant like I had no clue what they were really about. Gradually, I started gaining some interest, started underlining the important stuff, ended up making the page all red because everything seemed to be an important one to me, which was actually not the case. In reality I was just acting like I was grasping things, but that was still an alien part for me. I was pissed off by now and ended up almost tearing the data out in a fit of irritation. It was turning out to be the worst day in my professional life.

I just had one hope and that was Mridul, if he could do anything to save all of us from getting fucked by the presentation. Two hours since he had left for the Cat Lab and as the time was passing my hopes were reaching their heights assuming he must be working hard on the drawings, as I was hoped for the best Mridul came back shouting...

"Fuck man! It's not happening, we all are dead." He said.

"What? But you went to Cat lab."

"Yes, But it's impossible for us to make the drawings in one day."

"But what else we can do?"

"I don't know! I am pissed off."

"What happened guys?" Vipul said as he came in and saw Mridul and me talking in a tense voice.

Vipul is the head of Machines lab. He used to come for the latest collection of porn as our team was well known for it.

"Nothing man, Mr. Saini has asked us to prepare the presentation on the Escorts Project and you know the drawings. We haven't started it yet."

"Oh! I would say just go and hit Mr. Mishra's laptop. He must be having last year's drawings, I am sure."

"But you know that nerd. He will never reveal the stuff to me."

"Umm... Yeah, But you can give it a try or maybe you can hack his computer. But that's a big time job. Go for the first option."

"Anyways, Any new Stuff?"

The porn animal Vipul had given us light of hope, but we knew Mr. Mishra was never going to help us, just like he works on his own fundamentals and principals of life, a typical 50's boss. But still Mridul took a chance and went to his cabin but the story was the same. He didn't agree and all again we were on the same spot from where we started. I could see myself packing my bags and boarding the flight back to Delhi. Because failing in the project was going to be a big deal for the trainees. Frankly speaking, I was totally blank. I had no clue what to do, I don't know from where Kritika had appeared on my mind, as she was an ethical hacker before she joined the company.

"Kritika can help us." I said with no expressions but a hope.

"How?" Mridul sounded excited

"She was into ethical hacking before this job."

"Seriously? We must call her."

"No I can't do this. I am sorry. But this is not right." Kritika said.

"What? Kritika are you alright? You are saying no to me, your bestie!"

"I am saying no to hack someone's system."

"But if you do not do this, they will kick me out of the company. Imagine I won't be around you. You will be alone. Aren't you going to miss me?" I added, with a puppy face, full of emotional attyachar.

"Okay! Okay... Shut up, I will do it. But for the first and the last time."

"Okay done." Trying to hide my happiness.

Someone has truly said girls are emotional fools. And she was the best example of this. However, she had been a savior for us.

Hacking somebody is similar to fucking somebody, one term is physical and other is technical. In both you get the fun and pleasure, while the other gets hurt. And fucking.... Errrrrrrrr.... I mean hacking Mr. Mishra's computer gave us (Me and Mridul) a sheer pleasure, Courtesy: Genius Kritika. All the drawing layouts were right in front of us, no more tension. It was going to be good for us. All the material of presentation was there, only some editing was required which was really not a big deal, I expected Mridul to do it and he did. Some hours back we were afraid of getting fired, see how things changed rapidly; we just had a happy session hacking Mr. Mishra's laptop and next was to get the fuck out of presentation. It was fuck - fuck all around, with a background music puch puch.

"The expansion of gases caused by the heat from an exothermic chemical reaction results in a fore being applied to a movable component such as a piston. But here I would like to make a statement. If we increase the air gap there will be a considerable change in the efficiency of the machine." I said, rolling the last drawing sheet.

I felt like I was back in college where during practical exams I used to speak the most nonsensical things with sky high confidence and the teachers used to see me with the same disbelief ,these people expressed all over their faces. Only this time, because I was right or you can say I was good in copying things. Whatever it was, the bottom line was that we had just fucked the presentation.

"Very good team work Mridul, I appreciate it." Mr. Saini said looking at Mridul.

And finally by hook or crook we did it and it was party time now.

Archimedes declared that given a place to stand, he could move the earth. That's what engineers are. We can do everything, you want us to do, and all we need is time and resources.

"The Tsunami had come and now it left, let's get back to our regular work, you know what I mean." Mridul winked at me.

Our regular work consisted of browsing latest porn, face booking, glancing at every other girl in the accounts department, in short everything except drawing work.

SCARY NIGHT WITH FLAVOR OF BROKEN HEART

An E-Mail:

A helicopter was flying around above Bangalore when an electrical malfunction disabled the aircraft's electronic navigation and communications equipment.

Due to the clouds and haze, the pilot could not determine the location of the helicopter. He saw a tall building, flew toward it, circled it, and held up a handwritten sign that said 'WHERE AM I?' in large letters.

People in the tall building quickly responded to the message, drew a large sign, and held it up in window. Their sign said 'YOU ARE IN A HELICOPTER.'

The pilot smiled, waved, looked at his map, determined the course to steer to the Bangalore airport, and landed safely. After they were on the ground, the co-pilot asked him how he had done it.

"I knew it had to be the IT Park, because they gave me a technically correct but completely useless answer."

Mridul read the whole mail in one go and took a deep breath, but before the oxygen could even kiss his lungs Natasha's tube light brain acted like a street lamp and she got to know why he read it...

"So what do you exactly want to say, Mridul?" Natasha said in a taunting manner.

"As if you don't know baby!"

"NO! I don't know. Please elaborate."

"Nothing new. It's a technically entertaining joke on computer engineers."

"Ah! I mean your breed of engineers." He added and that added fuel to Natasha's angry mood which was soon going to erupt on him

"Oh! Really? You are about as entertaining as a child's inflatable punching toy. You bop it, it springs back, you bop it again and you forget it ever existed." Natasha said.

"Oh! Ahan? I didn't know that, Thanks for letting me know."

"I didn't know you are one confused lad, who aspired to become a lawyer in 8th grade, then a medico in 11th but ended up being thrown out of the school after 11 and eventually studying commerce in some dilapidated Govt. College. Your write-up testifies your plight. I simply sympathies you and pity you." And again Natasha made a statement which was just irrelevant like her every statement. Because this time she said all this without taking a break.

"Anything? No, I mean anything? At least get back on track baby."

"Whatever, I am not talking to you." And now her emotional attyachar took a great leap.

You gotta be rich to be insane... Losing your mind is not a luxury for the middle class and that too lovers. Ah! Especially for the breed called boy friend.

Oh! Jeez if you do so you are dead. After witnessing 'n' number of fights between Mridul and Natasha I can say this.

Most loves are like that; your heart starts to feel like an overcrowded lifeboat. You throw your pride out to keep it afloat and yourself respect and your independence after a while.

You start throwing people out, your friends, everyone you used to know and still it's not enough, the life boat is still sinking and you know it's going to take u down with it.

And the breaking news was that again Natasha left the place, but this time Mridul didn't give a damn. God knows why he didn't?

"There's no job for being right, there's no salary for knowing the truth and there's no fringe benefits for helping others." Mridul said.

"What do you mean?" I said, trying to grab the information he wanted to convey to us.

"Nothing you won't understand." He said.

Okay as you say. But I got to know the right and truth thing, what is this helping others part?"

"You will soon come to know." He gave me a mysterious smile.

Ah! Mridul and his mysterious looks. Sometimes, in fact most of the times they used to get me into trouble, I was just hoping this time it won't turn up like this. Because I was already pissed off about the things happening around me and last thing I wanted is to find myself into trouble.

"Don't worry Nick; I know what you are thinking." He said, grabbing his 3rd beer of the evening.

"Guilt is the hilt of the knife that we use on ourselves and love is often the blade, but its worry that keeps the knife sharp and worry that gets most of us in the end." I don't know why I said that, May be I was high and ended up being emotional.

"The sooner you fall behind, the more time you have to catch up." Kritika said, holding my hand, trying to give me support like always.

"No! The sooner you fall behind, farther you have to catch up and that is what I am doing."

"You need rest Nick." Mridul said in a teasing manner.

"What can motivate you in life? When you have had the best and it is gone forever." I said and the emotional ' ME ' was now again getting out of its shell.

"No, it's just what you want to feel. Remember Nick, We are able to walk on air, but only as long as our illusion supports us. So it's nothing but your illusion." Kritika again tried to boost me up and gripped my hand.

"Why can't you just leave it and move on?" Mridul said, irritated with my statements.

"Leaving everything behind, I moved ahead with time. Achieved everything I wanted, as never took anything for granted. Today I have everything but still nothing. But there is still something which lacks in me and makes me feel lonely in the crowd."

"Who said you are alone? Why don't you just throw your past away? You have got a better present." Kritika almost took me in her arms.

There are many things that we would throw away if we were not afraid that others might pick them up.

I don't know from where I was getting these philosophical thoughts. It was the height which was making me go insane. And the debate on this continued for next fifteen minutes. I was continuously trying to show my helplessness and Kritika was trying her best to get me out of this. But I knew somewhere this was just for the time being, because the intensity of Sneha's thoughts was very low, almost gone in my conscious state. It was my unconscious state which took me to such a situation.

"Oh! Shut the fuck up. I want something extremely sensational to happen now." Mridul said, trying to change the mood of the evening or in short trying to cut the crap of love and broken hearts.

"Something sensational, what's that now?" I asked

"Yes! Like rhythmic urination."

"What? Have you gone mad? What the hell is this now?"

"Let me explain, if you've ever pissed in an Indian style toilet you would know what rhythmical urination is. It begins with a sound that resembles that of a waterfall into an ocean or a river, not that loud of course, unless you are the Great Salastor himself, and then gradually the sound subsides just as the projectile of your urinary tract does." Mridul's this statement showed how funny character he was.

"Ah! You know what? It is disgusting just like you, But innovative too."

"Oh! Shut up. It's like so cheap." Kritika said, vomited her thoughts on Mridul.

"What else can you expect from my so called boy friend?" Natasha, Yeah! Yeah! She was back.

"Oh! Common if you cannot praise me then at least don't criticize me."

"Oh! My god, I am impressed... Bohhhoooo." Natasha said.

"Thank you so much baby, that is why I love you unconditionally." Mridul failed to understand the sarcasm in Natasha's statement.

"Awww... Anyways, why did you knock at the door?"

"Knock? I didn't. In fact none of us left our seat."

"Seriously? Stop kidding me."

"I swear! Oh my god. Is this happening again?"

"What?" Natasha sounded surprised.

It's about some six months ago, the moon has gone somewhere. I am scared of ghosts sometimes. I think of weird stuff, there is a house in our neighborhood, which is haunted. The cameras in the house have captured doors and windows opening and shutting automatically. A dog in that house fell down the stairs, police is investigating the case. I feel scared every night. But then I go underneath my quilt and just drown in the whirlpool of such thoughts and the comfort of my bed. And it is happening till date.

"Did dog fall down from stairs? Maybe the dog was drunk. You have to think that way, so that you won't feel afraid anymore." Kritika said, trying to calm the scary environment created by Mridul, and Natasha? I doubt if she had pissed in her pants. For the first time she didn't say anything, instead she took a seat on Mridul's lap.

"Yes but how can a dog fall like that down the stairs and die? I think some invisible force pushed it down. Yeah poor dog." Mridul said again.

"Oh! Shut up. Nothing like this can happen."

"How can you say that? I have felt this even when I was in Delhi."

"Oh! Really?" I said.

"2 years ago, one night around 12, there had been a mini earthquake in Delhi which lasted for 10 sec. But everything shook violently and I woke up suddenly. I felt it was the devil shaking the bed. I ran to my mum and that whole night I didn't let go of my mum." By the end of the statement Mridul couldn't hold back his laugh, looking at Natasha's face. For the first time she turned pale absolutely.

And we laughed out loudly.

"I will kill you, you scared me like hell." Natasha threw the cushion at me.

"Awww... Baby there is nothing like this. Okay, I am sorry."

"Sometimes sorry isn't enough, I just hate it. Kritika come with me, I am too scared to sleep alone now, Let these devils stay alone."

And they both went off to sleep and we continued with our conversation and drinking.

"I wonder why she has chosen to be an engineer." I said, referring to Natasha.

"Even I do."

"Well if an apple fell on her instead of Newton, the world would have got 3 laws of E-motion."

And again we got something to laugh about. Moreover she was not around so we were free now to do anything.

"Anyways, What about the girl from the drawing's department whom you were trying to be friendly with for the last two months."

"Oh! Avni? Well she is my heart and soul. But that Subramanian won't let that happen for much time."

"Why?"

"Because that jackass got to know about Natasha from somewhere, and he too likes Avni. So I suspect he will blackmail me soon."

"Oh! Sad."

"Anyways, cut the crap. Let's hit the sack, before that unknown power comes and hits us."

"What? You were serious?"

"You never know." He again winked at me.

"Oh! Man. You are a mystery for me."

And we went off to sleep. Before closing my eyes the thoughts of Sneha and Kritika flipped through my mind randomly. I thought of love, lust and life. And in the end it didn't even matter. That's what I got to know.

DANCE BAR PARTY ROMANCE

"Get up ... Get up... Get up Nick."

"NickkKkkkk....." And finally he kicked me, a kick on my ass.

It took me sometime, to realize that Mridul was trying to wake me up. I was almost taking it like a dream, He was shouting and like always, I did not give a fuck to his call until he gave a nasty kick on my ass and took me to the real world.

"What the hell! What do you want? Let me sleep." I said, irritated and pulled on the blanket again.

"Get up, its party time man." He said pulling off the blanket and throwing it on the table.

"No!! I am tired and in no mood to party."

Actually I was kind of bored with the same kind of schedule. Also that Kritika was turning out to be a boring companion to hang around with. Most of the times her chummy talks and emotional ones used to irritate me. I don't know why but she was taking care of me, which was okay. But pampering ewwwww!! I used to hate it like "Baby do this" and "Aww! My baby" and moreover nothing was really happening except the same boozing. Natasha's melodrama was kind of intolerable by now. Mridul's PJs had become boring by now. Obviously I was bored and fed up of the same old weekend parties.

"Are you sure? I thought you are going to love it."

"It? What's that?" rubbing my eyes.

"D... D... Dance Bar!" He winked at me.

"What? What is this? D... D... Dance bar?"

"Heaven!! Girls, girls... and more girls. Exposing their beautiful features. Letting you glance at them. Dancing for you surrounded by the lake of whiskey, river of beer and wells of Tequila. Flashing lights coming out of the smoke of weed."

"WTF! Stop kidding me."

"Okay, Your wish. You keep on rubbing your ass on this mattress but I am not going to spoil my Sunday, okay Nick?"

"No... Tell me... I mean, Grrrrr... Let's go ..."

"I knew my horny animal can never say no to this."

"But what about Natahsa and Kritika?"

"What about them? May be they are going to enjoy their dinner with rice and dal."

"What?"

"Yes, I have already told them that we are busy with the project today. So we can't join them."

"Good. Seriously it was all turning out to be a boring schedule. Now we need a change."

"And my dear here is the change, get ready. Remember dancing chicks are waiting for us." And he gave his mysterious smile.

We parked our car. While walking through the long row of shops around the corner, small doors, mostly wooden and carved, with some innocuous or sometimes suggestive board saying XYZ Restaurant. I was yet to come across a board "Dance Bar". Finally, I could see a uniformed bouncer standing at the door of the bar, I could hear the soft sound of Hindi film music in the distance.

The man at the door had the discretion to let you enter or stop you there. But in our case he welcomed us with a warm handshake and an equally warm greeting. Maybe he had seen potential boozers with lot of money. The door opened. Suddenly, we found ourselves in a soundproof corridor, and one of the men at the door took us through it. It opened into the darkened dance bar. The chamber welcomed us with a deafening noise.

I could see that I was at one end of an atrium, with reclining sofas and seats spread close to the walls, a dance floor in the middle and girls dancing. There were seats strategically closer to the dance floor where one could have a better view of the dancers. In any case, it didn't matter where you sat because as long as you were stuffed with cash, the dancers would come to you. That I could make out in the first five minutes. The performing girls were clad in traditional ghagra cholis and navel-revealing skirts, low-cut blouses and colorful accessories. There was little about them that I could find vulgar. And to the music of thumping Hindi film songs, they performed what went under the name of dance.

Of course we preferred to sit closest to the dance floor. While I was wondering, "How many of these people had I met before?" I wondered. A moment later, my gin and tonic slid in front of me, and the bartender was gone before I could even look up to mouth the words Thanks. "Wouldn't have mattered anyway." Mridul mused, as it is clearly understood that one speaks of gratitude with cash, not words.

The dances were pathetic, to say the least. Very few of girls could really dance. Most of them were just shaking their hips and bodies pretending. The more they tried to make it look better, the more pathetic it seemed. But yeah, the shaking act of the girls around, cleavage showing was pumping my hormones. With every sip of tonic, I could feel it.

Ah! The way she was looking at me. Damn, Every time, she glanced at me, Every time, I felt the hardness. But like always, she had her eye on the cash I had in my pocket. I must say, the place was perfect for jilted lovers, desperate oldies who were bored with the same old sex life, desperate teenagers who always had fantasies of looking into deep cleavages the bar catred to all.

The "dance" was accompanied by a shower of money. One can walk up to their favorite dancer and shower her with money. There is no limit as to how much money one can throw.

"Man, I love it. Thanks for bringing me to this heaven."

"What about that girl in a red saree, isn't she hot?" Mridul said, pointing at one of the dancers in red.

As he beckoned her she came and sat just next to me. Oh! She touched me, teased me, passed her hand over my face, Ah! That was enough to make me shower all my money on her, I had in my pocket. She smiled at me, gave a lil kiss on my cheek. Oh! Oh! It was heavenly...

"Calm down Nick, go slow." Mridul said, making me come to reality.

"Oh! Shut up, you are just jealous that she approached me."

"Really? Wait." He said.

As he showed a bunch of notes to her and she came to him and did the same... Oh! We were kind of enjoying it, but the cost of all the pleasure was high, So before we got carried away, we decided to move out of the place. Moreover the showering was enough for the day and without it, one could never get any favors. The way the dancers were teasing us, we were sure, that if we stayed on even half an hour, we would be dead.

As we came out of the dancing heaven, obviously we were high and flying.

"Okay, so what's next?" I said.

"Ummm... I am kind of missing Natasha." he said.

"Oh! Hello... I asked what's next. Mr. Romeo."

"Yeah! I am missing her."

"What? You have gone insane, you are so high."

"Okay you drive but ..."

"But what?"

"Drive to Divesh Enclave."

"What?"

"Yes I feel like hugging her tightly."

"Man... you have gone mad."

And finally we drove to Natasha's place that's in Divesh Enclave, Two nerds. High on beer - whiskey - gin, smoke.

"Stop - Stop!" Mridul resting his left leg on the car window.

"What now?" pulling of the breaks, irritated.

"I want to present her with a rose, a red one." Giggles.

"What the fuck! Now from where the hell we get a rose?"

"Rose garden where else?"

"Don't act insane Mridul. It's midnight and mind you there is a hell of security there."

"So what? I have a plan."

"Cool... So what's the plan?"

"Listen. It's very simple; the fencing of the rose garden is not that high. We can jump over it and pluck the rose for my rosy."

"Oh! Very simple, right? STFU."

After some 20 minutes of argument, Mridul finally succeeded convincing me to go with his fucking lunatic plan. As we reached the place, I decided to go alone; As Mridul was finding it difficult even to stand straight. The fencing of the garden was not that high. I jumped in and instead of plucking one rose, I plucked two. The thought of Kritika came to my mind and I felt that she would feel special if I gave her a rose as well. As I was just thinking I heard a voice in the distance saying "Hey! Who is there? Stop ..." Darn! It was the security guard. I ran out and with two three falls, passing the hurdle, and fencing. I finally escaped from there.

"Take this and now don't dare to say anything." I said gathering my lost breath.

He kissed me on the cheek which was so ugh and said, "Thank you darling, you are my bestie."

A guy - guy bestie thing is only if they are drunk which our case was or if they are gay. This is actually the theory of most of the people around. If a girl is holding another girl's hand – the reaction would be - "Awww! so sweet" and if two guys do the same - reaction would be - Ugh! Gays. Right?

We reached the place, the girls were waiting outside. Mridul had already informed them that we were coming. Kritika was wearing black silk night wear, hairs falling down. She looked to me more beautiful than ever. I came out and ignoring Natasha and Mridul I went to her and smiled in a wicked manner.

"What? Are you alright Nick?" Kritika showed me some concern.

"Yes perfectly." I fumbled twice to say it perfectly.

"Ahan? I can see that baby."

"This is for you." I gave her the rose.

"Awwww... Thank you so much."

A silent walk along the street. I looked at her and she did the same. After ten steps, I felt the touch of her fingers on my hand. She rested her hand over mine, then gripping it hard. I was high but I could feel that the unspoken thoughts that she wanted to share desperately with me gave her a high as well. But was I interested in knowing them? Was I aware of those feelings? Was I trying to ignore them as my first experience was not that heartening.. Was I? Was ... I? I don't know what it was but that short walk was a special one.

"Thank you for the rose Nick." She said looking at it again.

"Just thank you?"

"What else do you want?" She winked at me.

"You know it."

She wrapped her arms round my neck and whispered, "Okay Nick."

"No... Closer." I said in a low voice.

She came a little closer to me but there was still an air gap between us

"More closer "

Obeying my command she snuggled against me. I could feel her breath, maybe she felt mine. The fragrance of her hair was so mesmerizing. I was losing control on myself and she was just melting in my arms. I pushed her against the wall, held her arms above her head and kissed her. I bit, licked and rolled all over her tongue and finally she pulled back and stood there silently. I tried to make eye contact with her but she looked down. I planted a kiss on her forehead. She smiled at me and said, "I always knew you are a good kisser, but you surprised me you are so passionate." I gave her a wicked smile but before we could continue I heard Mridul calling me from the corner of the street.

"Nick!! Where the hell are you?"

"Why are you shouting?" I said.

"Let's go." He was already waiting for me in the car.

Breaking News: Natasha and Mridul had one more fight. Natasha was not there and the reason was the emotional Mridul told her everything about the evening when we had gone to a dance bar, expecting her to react normally seriously he was a dumb ass. Every time I tried to go closer to Kritika, Mridul was there to spoil everything. I hated him for that.

AND.... WTF?

R.O.F.L.S.H.T.E.T.I.G.U.I.F.D.A.H.M.B.O.T.A.T.L, rolling on the floor so hard that every time I got up I fell down again hit my head on the table and I almost turned lunatic.

"Are you serious Man?" I said.

"YES!! He has gone crazy." Dev said.

Rolling on the floor describes my state of amusement, although it seemed to be a weird one. When Dev told me, "Harsh is going to marry." It was like what the fuck? How can he?

"He could have got engaged, But Marriage? Damn, don't you think he is calling his death to doorsteps? Death of his independence."

"Yeah Exactly, Anyways, there is one more news for you."

"Oh! Don't tell me you too planning such an idiotic thing."

"STFU... Will you? I am talking about the reunion, college reunion party."

"Oh yeah, I saw the event on Facebook."

"So are you coming?"

"Most probably; let's see if it works."

"Oh come on man! Come, we guys miss you. And more over it's been six months now, you can get a one week vacation."

"I am checking the tickets."

"Okay cool, Anyways, Mom's calling. I will call you later and don't forget to get my present."

"Oh sure, take care."

How life had changed! One of my best friends was going to marry. But he was lucky I guess, at least he got the girl whom he loved. According to him, he was doing what he and his girl friend wanted. What else did he want? A happy family. Oh! Happy family, two turning three then four in the next three years and by the time of my marriage Harsh would be the perfect uncle leading a sedate life.

"Congratulations, your leave application has been approved." Mridul said as he threw the envelop almost at my face.

"Oh Really!"

"Yes, but just for one week."

"Oh yeah, it's enough."

"Anyways, did you get your tickets booked?"

"No! I was waiting for the leave to be granted first."

"Holy fuck! Are you insane or what?"

"Calm down! I still have 5 days. I will get it."

"Hope so. Anyways, Nick there is something I want to say to you. Don't mind but it is serious. Can we do it right now?" I had never seen such an expression on his face except once when I caught him shagging.

"Oh sure." Confused me.

"I want to talk to you about Kritika I guess she loves you and as far as I know you will never go for relationships again, then why don't you just tell her everything, instead of showing affection to her publicly. Nick you to know she is a very good girl. Let's not hurt her, by giving her false hopes."

"Yes, But I don't really know if she loves me or not. May be it's just an infatuation. Yes I like the way she cares for me, even I feel like caring for her but just as a bestie."

"Infatuation?"

"Yes, now shut up and cut the crap. Let me look for my ticket."

"When will you stop behaving like a kid? Running away from problems!"

"Next month, I promise. Now shut up please."

Yes I was running away from things. First, because I was scared of falling in love again and getting hurt. Second, I had never thought about Kritika that way, more than a friend, I was scared.

Next... Next.... Information... Confirm... Print.....!!!

Phewww! I got my ticket booked. Though it cost me a lil' more, but compared to the fun in Delhi a few thousand bucks were kind of minimal. Moreover I desperately needed a break from the same routine I had faced for the six months. Sometimes, I used to wonder, what I actually wanted. Six months back, I desperately wanted an escape from Delhi and now I wanted a break from Bangalore. I was unstable. I never knew what I wanted. After sometime I needed a break or whenever I find myself beset by problems, I used to run away from problems and always tried to find an easy escape from them. I was going back home, I was happy. This thought unnerved me somewhat for the first time in six months.

"I am going back home on Sunday, Kritika."

"What?" Shocked as if I had told her that I was pregnant.

"Yes, what happened? Shocked?"

"Damn! How can you? I mean.... You didn't even tell me."

"Actually, everything just happened all of a sudden."

"WTF? What do you mean by all of a sudden?"

"Calm down! I am just going for one week."

"OH! Then it's okay." She finally smiled.

"Phewww!"

"But I will miss you." That was so sweet of her.

"Now stop acting like an Emotional Queen and smile."

"Hehehe..."

"No, That devilish one."

"Khi – Khi." She giggled.

"I said devilish not rubbish."

"HoooohahahahahaaaBahahawahaha ...." Everyone in the coffee shop turned to look at her but she looked cutely at me.

Bags packed - All set. Mridul, Natasha and Kritika came to see me off at the airport. Mridul with his big brother lecture and Kritika with her emotional attyachar, for a moment I felt like leaving the place without saying goodbye. Everything was turning out to be so tense and unbearable as if I was leaving forever or I was going to die.

"Can't you guys behave normally?" I said.

I hugged them and as I was leaving Kritika gave me a folded letter and asked me to open it once I was on board.

CHAPTER: BACK TO HOME

As soon as I settled down in the plane, I thought of opening the letter which Kritika had given me. I don't know why but I was curious. I kind of knew that it would be some good luck message, typical girlish stuff or may be some Mantras as Kritika believed strongly in horoscopes and mantras. Still I was dying of curiosity to see what was in it. I was about to to unfold it when the hostess came with some DVDs. Ah! I didn't like any one of them. While travelling I mostly prefer to plug in my I pod rather than going for those melodramatic Hindi movies, which you get in jet planes.

The letter had almost seven folds. Like she had just passed me some top secret of FBI, Finally I started unfolding it. First... Second......... Seventh and It was........

Hello Nick,

I want to say something to you. Tried to say it many times but really couldn't. So I am trying to say it now.

Since we met, I can say honestly that I have loved every minute we have spent together! I mean it. It's been wonderful. I find myself liking you more and more each time we talk. You have the ability to make me feel happy about myself, about the funny little things in life... but mostly just about being with you because it's a very good place to be. I am lucky I met you and I want you to know just how great I think u are.

I don't know if you have any feelings for me, but Nick "I love you ". Can I love you forever?

I will wait for your reply.

Miss you

Kritika.

I ended up smiling because it always feels good knowing that someone loves you so much and Ah! That was the first time for me. The first time someone loved me I had no clue what to do. Thank god she expressed her feelings through a letter not face to face. Do I feel the same for her? No - Yes - No.

I was confused rather I was scared. I am strong because I am weak. I am okay because I know my flaws. I am a lover because I am a fighter. I am fearless because I have been afraid. I am wise because I have been foolish. And I can laugh because I have known sadness with the letter sent shivers through my body. After Sneha left me I had started hating the idea of love. For me there was no love and life was all about lust. The only good thing was that she gave me one week to think about it. But was one week enough to take such a big decision? To turn myself into a lover boy again? May be no, because my past experience had taught me that there was nothing called love and if it did exist, it really was a dirty business.

"I am right now feeling really weird and have these mixed thoughts... on one hand is my life...which has no beginning no end... the other side there is this person who seems to bind me and keeps going in circles, says she loves me and ends up not having any other commitment but love. Is that what love really is? I feel lost... I am starting to think negatively. Or is it just another phase in my life, can't think straight.

Yes Kritika had worked wonders for me to get the smile back on my face. She always made me feel special and turned up as my bestie. But does that mean I needed to love her? I had turned up as a feeling less man or maybe I was pretending to be one. It was my fear of getting hurt again which was holding me back. And without thinking any more about it, I placed it on hold and folded the letter again and put it back in my pocket. I had a week to think about it.

My flight landed in Delhi at around 6 pm. Ah! Peak office hours. It was just what I had expected. Uncontrolled traffic, mad beggars around, open sewage tanks. But all this really provided me the feeling of coming back home. From the organized Bangalore to the disorganized capital city Delhi.

There was dramatic change in the behavior of mom and dad towards me. Especially dad, who always took me as a spoiled unused brain was more considerate. I could see proud of me as he asked me questions about my job. And mom, Ah! I guess she had spent the last three nights in kitchen, like she had prepared everything which I like Dad's eyes shone with pride.The moment he saw me and Mom had tears of happiness. She hugged me.

"So how's the Job?" Dad asked.

"It's good, great experience."

"I always wanted you to join the family business but I am now happy that you took a step forward and decided to stand on your own."

"I am proud of you son." He added.

"Oh! Thank you dad."

I never knew that a '25 K' job could bring so much happiness to them. I was always busy in satisfying my own needs. It was just me, mine and myself. Never gave a thought as to how my mom dad would be feeling seeing their son spoiling his life in college. Though now it was all changed, though I still booze and smoke but in addition to that. I had started paying intentional or unintentional attention towards my career. Not only them, I had managed to get attention and respect from neighbors and relatives as well, I could see mom and dad feeling proud of me as they never had expected me to do something or rather anything in life.

"Mom this is for you." I gave her the pearl necklace which she really liked and the credit goes to Kritika because she was the one who chose it and for dad, I got a Van Husan blue shirt. He too liked it because it was his favorite brand and color. Yes, I acted little smart in this move.

After a little chit chat with mom and answering dad's queries regarding the job, I went to my room. Ah! I had been missing my bed. Its then that I actually got the feeling of 'being home '. The fragrance of the room bought the special feeling to me. I was exhausted by then, thought of taking a nap but like always, Mr. irritating aka Mr. Sleep spoiler, Dev came. For the first time I didn't feel like giving a hard kick on his ass for not letting me sleep because I had really missed this dumb fucker. I hugged him but more than my hug he was interested in seeing what there was in my bag for him.

"What's up?" Dev said getting over my new bed sheet and almost raping and crushing it.

"Nothing ya, Hell tired."

"To hell with that, tell me where my gift is?"

"Oh! Now a greedy dog is coming to the point."

"Yes. Of course, so before I start barking or bite you, give me my bone, I mean my gift."

"You know what? You are still an asshole."

"Oh yes I am!"

"Okay, it's in the side pocket, go and get it."

Mom called me downstairs to introduce me to our new neighbors. It took hardly five minutes and as I came back to my room I saw....

"What is this Nick?" Dev said with a damn serious expression holding the letter which Kritika had given me .

"Oh Jesus! From where the hell did you get it? Give it to me."

"Oh! Shut up and tell me."

"It's none of your business, so kindly STFU."

"Okay Cool, You don't want me to know who Kritika is and all but by reading this letter I can surely make out that she loves you a lot and as far as I know you, I am sure that you are not going around with her. Yes you must be scared after all that happened between you and Sneha. But man I want to say that every girl is not the same. Of course it's your life you know what's good for you."

"Oh! Common, Stop acting like a love guru. Anyways, not a bad lecture Mr. Dev Khurana."

"Oh! Thank you."

"Something fishy ... Some one's in love I guess." I said. I could make out the way he was talking.

"Well! I am cooler, first fill me up with beer, and then you can take anything out of me. Till then Shhhhh..."

"Okay."

Well! I could see a real change in Dev; I didn't know what it was. But in the first thirty minutes I could make out that he had become a lot more sincere regarding love. Whatever the reason might be, but it was a welcome change in him. The way he said 'every girl is not the same kind of 'stuck in my mind.

CHAPTER: CONFESSION!

"I told you..... I told you....."

"She always had deep feelings for you."

"Oh! Common Nick, You always knew this is going to happen someday."

"Stop being a loser."

Mridul called me up and I told him the whole story of the love letter which Kritika had given me. When I told him about my fear of getting hurt again and apprehension about love, he gave his respective reactions. Before leaving Bangalore, Mridul had a talk with me regarding Kritika but then like now, I was trying to run away from it. Yes I liked Kritika, I could never deny it. My mind and my past experience was not allowing me take a step forward.

"Can I ask you something?" Mridul said.

"Yes."

"Are you still attached to Sneha?"

"No!! I don't even hate her, because hatred is also a feeling but I feel nothing for her."

"Then, why don't you move on man?"

"I have moved on but that doesn't mean I need to love someone."

"Yes you need to. See Sneha left you, maybe that happened for something good and see now Kritika is waiting for you. You can't deny that you like her."

"Yes I do, but I don't have any feelings because I know love is really a dirty business."

"Listen Nick! I can't change your mind. But lastly I would say, every girl is not the same, and you yourself know that how much Kritika loves you. Somewhere at the back of your mind you too have feelings for her, you can't run away from that."

"Correction, I don't have any. I told you earlier too."

"Okay, Whatever, But do give it a second thought."

"I will."

"Anyways, how's everything going on? I hope you are enjoying every bit of VIP treatment."

"Oh God! How do you know that?"

"Common Nick! I know how family members pamper you, when you go back home after such a long time."

"Exactly, Dramatic change isn't it?"

"I know! Anyways, enjoy yourself and do give a second thought to it. I will call you later, Natasha is calling me."

He hung up...

Mridul's words made a deep impact on me. I started thinking about the whole thing but I was still scared of getting hurt and though I said I didn't have any feelings for Sneha, I lied to him. Somewhere in my heart she still had a secure place. I was kind of still stuck to her, though the intensity was very very low.

I was absolutely lost in my thoughts and forgot that Dev was waiting for me inside for the next peg of antiquity. As I went in, Dev was busy on his phone and Ah! Darn... He had finished almost half the bottle and poor me, who was thinking that he had been waiting for me.

He took ten more minutes to finish his call. As soon as he was done, I shouted at him; "Are you insane or what?"

"What?"

"You are half down man and with whom were you talking?"

"Oh! Cut the crap. I need to talk to you."

The moment he said that he needed to talk to me, I was hoped he wouldn't throw his bloody lecture on love at me because I was totally pissed off by now with the same kind of talks and lectures, as if these guys have no other work than settling my love life. But when he spoke it was altogether on a different matter.

"Yeah say?" I said.

"Nick I am in love."

"Seriously? Man this is news for me." I almost fell off my chair.

"Yes." Emotional and sad face, Dev.

"What happened? Why aren't you happy? Damn you should feel lucky that you got the one. Oh! Don't tell me your story is the same as that of mine."

"No! She is far better than Sneha."

"Ahan? You mean to say she is some goddess of hotness."

"Oh! Shut up."

"No, you yourself said she is better than Sneha, So I thought you are sad because she is too hot to handle."

"Oh come on Nick! For me the real beauty is not the woman's physical appearance, it's in her heart where beauty lies."

"Oh! I see. But then what's the problem."

"Actually it's complicated; first promise me you won't laugh."

"Complicated? Yeah that's expected from you. Oh! Come on. You are my best friend, how can I laugh at you." The later line depicted that I was also feeling high by now and emotional Nick was getting out of the shell.

"Actually we met on a social networking site."

"WTF? Net love, Eh?"

"Yeah, we met on Face Book and used to chat for hours and hours."

"Okay."

"But she never showed me her picture."

"Oh! Blind love? Very Complicated."

"You can say that, but I never felt like asking her for the picture, because the real beauty was unseen, untouchable but I could feel it. For me the real beauty was not physical appearance, it was in her heart. with unconditional love and tender care to someone special. And I started feeling for her."

"Then?"

"Today she sent me her real picture."

"Oh! Awesome Can I see it?"

And showed me her picture on his phone

She looked like a cute girl with big specs but there was innocence in her smile and face was adorable. She was not ugly but you could not call her beauty queen. She seemed to be an innocent girl with high values. I didn't know how to react. What to say to Dev? Because if you ask me, I would say Dev deserved a hot enchanting beauty, but the change which this innocent angel had brought in this horny animal. Dev seemed to be more serious, emotional and in addition to that he had started valuing the relationship. So at the cost of all these valuable things beauty was negotiable and moreover she had bought a smile to his face, so I was happy for him.

"So you didn't like her."

"No dumb head, I told you earlier too for me physical beauty hardly matters."

"Then what's the fucking problem?" I scratched my head.

"The problem is regarding her, she feels that I will ditch her as she is not beautiful. Actually she is an insecure person."

"Oh!"

"But I am going to make her realize how much I love her. She should not feel insecure as I love only her."

"My lover boy, I can't believe you are the same irritating soul."

"Shut up."

Like always that night we drank like hell. In between Kritika called me up but I didn't take her call. It was not that I didn't want to talk to her, but I was just running away from her.

CHAPTER: (REUNION)

Ah! The college reunion. The first reunion weekend at college cafeteria, of course there was no better place to reunite. It seemed as though everyone was either jobless, still struggling to complete the degree or getting engaged or married. Because I did not belong to any of these categories, I had to look my best and impress them, pleasant with some amazing life update. I had job. Now I just needed a killer wardrobe to wow my friends, piss off my frenemies and entice all the girls around. Ah! I was hoping for too much, but someone has said, 'Think big' so here I was.

I went to college with sky high confidence which I had never experienced earlier. Maybe it was my success in professional life that bought it up. With a feel of kicking ass of those who had thought I was a loser and with the curiosity of meeting some nice ones.

But all the stunts I thought of got dissolved in emotions as soon as I entered the campus, I found myself lost in memories. The memories of college life we used to live. Every single thing around reminded me of the time that I had spent there. Though at the time of farewell I had thought my college life was not that eventful, but now coming back to the place made everything look absolutely fresh and mesmerizing. While walking on the road from the parking area to the cafeteria, my mind was lost somewhere. Looking at the present students on the basketball court mainly known as the lovers point reminded me of those times when Sneha and I used to spend hours and hours there talking and teasing each other. I felt like capturing every single moment in my camera.

The cafeteria, the place where I had spent most of my time seemed to be the same. The fragrance of freshly prepared meals was still there. I took a deep breath and tried to in hail the same fresh air of the place where I used to spend hours and hours. In my college days I had never felt like I was wasting time in cafeteria. In fact for me it was the most wonderful place on the campus. I tried to get the feel of every single moment I had spent there. In the last six months, I had been so busy with the battle of my new life that I never gave a thought to what would be happening around here. That's why people say nothing stops and things do move on. I had moved on but looking back, I could feel each and every moment I had spent here, memories related to the place. I thought that only reason people held onto memories was because memories were the only thing that didn't change when everything else did.

Meeting all the batch mates or class mates with whom I spent the most wonderful and valuable four years of my life was great. We discussed things which life had taught us, sharing the success stories, gossiping about bosses, secret love stories etc. It hardly took ten minutes for people to warm up with each other I could smile by myself but together we laughed and celebrated being together.

That was the time to enjoy the meet and remember the old days.

Rahul Bose sang to his own funny music.

Abhishek enthralled everyone with his distinguished voice.

Vinay's juggling amused everyone.

"Okay now Mr. Bunker Nick will say something." Dev said.

"I was more of an 'Attender' than a bunker." I said

Prashant and Harsh had a big laugh over my effort not to get into trouble.

Refreshing the memories I took alone walk on the long road from cafeteria to lecture hall. With every step, I could see every single picture right in front of me. What I used to do.... What we used to do... What it was ... What it is now...?

Looking at the road side bench I could still feel the pain what I felt on those last days. How she left me, I was so much lost, Lost in memories.

I don't know if I should smile or laugh. I moved on. I took a step forward like I have moved on in life leaving everything behind. I heard a voice from the back "*Nikhil Arora Bread Ka Pakora*"

Well! That's what Sneha used to call me and No doubt, it was Sneha, I turned around and she was right in front of me. The situation which I always wanted not to come across, the frame of life which I wished to skip was right there. I never wanted to face Sneha again in my life after she left me. But look at destiny; it had dragged me to such a situation. Sneha, Same road and ten meters away from the bench. Though she was looking as beautiful as ever she was wearing a black Guess tee that had a big and bold Guess written on it and her skinny Levis was still showing off her shapely figure, that a zillion of guys would go mad for. She had a broad smile on her face with perfect dimples and rosy lips like always, beautiful but dangerous. But the change for the moment was that despite of all such features, despite of the fact that she was right in front of me, I felt nothing. I went numb, with a straight face, no real expression.

"Look who is here." She said and took a step forward.

Was that a step forward to my life?

"Hey Hi." I said, took a pause "Long time."

"Yes long time, you seem to have changed." She said and asked me if she could join me for a walk.

I nodded.

"So how are you Junior Engineer?" She said.

"How do you know?"

"I don't stalk, I investigate."

"Anyways, I am doing well in fact I am awesome."

"Oh! Great, so cherishing the old memories."

"Yes some good.... some bad."

"I know later part turned bad, courtesy me." She looked down.

"Not really, that was just a part and parcel of life." I tried to act strong.

"No, I feel sorry for myself and I still have regrets." She said.

"Regrets? About what?" I tried to look surprised...

"About that night, how everything got changed. How insane I was!"

"Oh Come on!"

"No! I swear I missed you, I am glad to see you again."

"Oh! Really?"

"Yes, I even tried to call you but your Delhi number was switched off, tried to contact you on Facebook, but I guess I am blocked from there."

WTF? One more story. For many days, two hundred and seventeen to be precise, she had not bothered to keep in touch. Then suddenly one day she walks up to me to ask me something. Was she saying all this? Had she really missed me? My heart said yes, but my mind... Ah! My mind went blank, I had nothing to say. I kept quiet and silently listened to her. Oh! Wait... Wait... Was I dreaming? Unfortunately I wasn't. It was all happening in real; She was standing right in front of me and was confessing her feelings for me. But why now? Why? Where was she when I was alone?When I was fighting for my existence? Where was she when I was crying? Now when everything seemed perfect for me, a satisfying life, she came up to the scene. She kept talking for 20 minutes and I was silent, though I had so many questions to ask her I kept quite. I was just wondering where my destiny had dragged me. I just had one question, why? She had asked for my number. I didn't know if I really wanted to be with her now or not.

"Well! I am yet to take a new number, you give me yours, and I will call you." I said, though I had my phone in my pocket like the rose which I had wanted to give her on farewell night.

She took a slip out and gave me her number saying, I will wait for your call."

"Oh sure. Well! I have to take leave now, Dev and the others are waiting for me." I said and left the place. This time I didn't look back like the day she had left me and I had been still on my knees.

But the question was, whether I was going to come back to her. On one side the love of my college life love was waiting for me and on the other it was Kritika who was waiting for my reply.

It seems when you want someone they don't want you and when someone wants you, you don't want them and when you want each other something has to come and mess it up.

I love you. That's what she said when we lay together in her bed, the sheets twisted and hot. Her naked flesh slid over mine, and her teeth were as sharp as razors. She cut me with her fingernails and bit me. She fancied herself a vampire, and she was beautiful. She could easily be one. If only she wasn't so rotten inside. If only she wasn't so insane.

I don't know why it happened. I don't know when or how. I just know that it did. She came into my life, poisoning it, seeping its darkness into my veins like a hydraulic needle. Drip. Drip. I think I might just have to leave the heater on tonight, locking the doors and windows. I'll kiss her bloody lips once more, and leave. Because I just don't want her to come back and hit my feelings and heart again like she did long ago. I just don't want to be in the same state. I don't have strength in my knees anymore and my eyes are also not that strong to look back and see her going away from me, Oh! I simply don't trust you Sneha.

I remember a time when she was not so bitter. When she did not hide behind a mask, when she did not pretend to be someone else. But that was long ago, so so long ago. Her secrets are rotted skeletons in the darkest of closets and her memories are hanging on meat hooks in the coldest of refrigerators. I don't like speaking of my past now, it haunts me, torments me. She hides behind many faces, pretending to be someone else.

I felt the weight coming on to my shoulders again. Somehow somewhere I knew that I was going wrong. Seemed as if I was messing up my own life. Playing with my own emotions still I cringe at the thought. Is it okay to cheat my feelings or is it better to suppress them into my soul. I wish I could find the last piece in this puzzle. It looks so empty without its piece. I know I have it in one of my pockets but I guess I am too lazy to put it back where it belongs.

LUV IS A DIRTY BUSINESS?

For myself:

Everything has been going fine, I don't have a reason in this world to get stuck to you, the wrong ones that life throws have decreased, even the answers to all those weird sums is coming out to be right. My hair has grown long enough again, my discarded hair band has come back, I am not sad and not really very happy, no more bouts of insanity, I am feeling quite sane, peaceful, enjoying the chirping of birds around me.

But somewhere a feeling of long existing pain still lingers. I don't know what this is about; I don't know why I see darkness, when everything seems so bright.

For Sneha :

Lost you long ago, and don't want to get you back again. Please don't appear in my dreams again, because it hurts so much, now I don't feel anything for you. You were the one who made me insane. You left my heart bruised; now I don't want that bitchy life you stole. I feel lost, and fooled. I cried, I got torn. But now I am all mine. I want you to feel that pain.

You must be thinking you won, but girl you lost me. Feel the pain. Don't worry about me. When you were gone, I started afresh and believe me, it's all fine. It's really fine, even better now, I got myself back, somehow I am alone, I am content now, nothing more to repent. Sometimes it pains deep inside, still I retain all my pride to stay tall no more thinking about you.

For Kritika:

I am sorry it had to end like this. I am sorry that I can't be what you want me to be. I am sorry that loving me caused you so much hurt. I am sorry that I have done nothing but exacerbate your insecurities.

I am sorry that I walked into your life, gave you hope and not fulfilling your dreams. I am sorry!!

I am not sorry that I met you. I am not sorry that I liked you. I am not sorry for letting you come into my life where no one was allowed. I am not sorry for loving you with all my being while I could. I am not sorry for having felt wonderfully loved and cherished at the expense of your insecurities.

Your life, my life will go on. With a big hole that would take a long time to fill. With hurt that will take a long time to heal. With hope that one day the pain would ease and eventually go away.

My feelings for you will never go away….. And that is a promise. I never meant to hurt you the way I know I have.Your love means more to me than anything and I'll do whatever it takes to prove that to you. Since the day I met you and your love touched my heart I knew that my life would never be the same.

Please forgive me for the pain I have caused.

I will make it up to you.

You will remain my Best friend!

And life goes on... Yes! I love you, but can't make you feel that. Because I know "LOVE IS A DIRTY BUSINESS "

But still I would like to do it again.